STILL HEALING

A SPICY LATER IN LIFE ROMANCE SERIES

STILLWATER SPRINGS
BOOK THREE

JEM JOHNSON

THOSE JOHNSON GIRLS

CHAPTER ONE

"Lord help me. He's doing it again."

I didn't need to look up from my work to know what my second-best friend in the whole world was referring to. We were finally done with the setup for the Stillwater Spring Fair. The booths were in place, the pie tables covered, the lights strung—and if a few of the decorations looked suspiciously familiar, well... they were.

Some of the bunting came straight from the Town Jubilee, which had taken place last fall, and the wreaths had definitely made an appearance at the Christmas Market just a few months ago. Stillwater loved any excuse to celebrate. Mostly because it meant everyone could gather in one place, nibble on something sugary, and catch up on who was doing what with whom.

Celia was tying and retying the same bow on the welcome banner as she watched *him* doing the *thing* again. Lana, my first best friend in the whole world, was pretending not to supervise the two of us. And I was practicing my favorite illusion: serenity.

Across the green, Zach McNaulty stood with Belle Porter near the art tent. Even from here, the difference between them was blatant. Belle, perfectly put together, sunshine and charm; Zach, tall and uncertain, his hands tucked into the pockets of jeans that had seen better days.

"You think our boy is going to get anywhere with her this time?" Lana asked, grabbing a pretzel from a half-empty bag and popping it into her mouth like it was popcorn at a movie show.

I noted the use of the term *our boy*. Though Zach was Celia's son, he belonged to all of us in that way when girlfriends were closer than their siblings and we became honorary aunties. It was the same way with Lana's kids. I had been Aunt Tess for over two decades. I'd spoiled each and every one of Lana's girls, so much so that they'd often come to me with their problems instead of going to their mother. But that wasn't the case anymore. Not now that their mom had cut the proverbial umbilical cord, and the girls were finally solving their own problems themselves.

"You think she's into him?" Lana asked around a mouthful of salt and flour.

Celia groaned. "She's smiling, but that's a polite smile. It's her mother's smile."

"Belle is not her mother," I coaxed, but Celia didn't hear me. The ghost of Billie Davis Porter haunted Celia on a daily basis.

It didn't matter that Billie's husband had only had eyes for Celia since they were kids. Because Billie had interloped in Celia and Bo's childhood friends to lovers story and made herself the heroine. Billie had married Bo Porter when Celia failed to mount a horse and rescue her hero from the wicked witch of her love story. Now that the witch was vanquished, resting peacefully after what I knew had been a good life with Bo and their daughter, Billie still haunted Celia from time to time. Celia needed to get over her fixation on Billie getting there first, especially when she was now in possession of her happily ever after with her Prince Charming.

"That's a please stop talking before I die of secondhand embarrassment smile," Celia was saying.

I tried to see what she meant. Belle had a soft,

sunshine look about her. Her eyes crinkled, head tilted just enough to make any boy believe he was the reason light existed. She did look a little like her mother in this light. But Belle was actually nice, not fake nice like Billie had been.

Though Billie had always been nice to me. But that was only because her quarterback boyfriend hadn't been stealing glances at me when she was talking to him over milkshakes.

Belle wasn't stealing glances at anyone else. But she wasn't giving Zach much more than polite attention, either. Snatches of their conversation floated across the lawn.

"I meant to tell you," Belle said, holding her phone toward him. "That rendering you did of the downtown renovation? It's stunning. My clients couldn't stop talking about it."

Zach blinked, as if he'd forgotten how to take a compliment. "You really think so?"

"I know so." Belle tucked a strand of hair behind her ear, still smiling. "You made my job easy. It's like you saw what I was trying to say before I did."

I saw it happen in slow motion. Zach's entire posture changed; chest opening, face lighting. Confidence, delicate and new, blooming right there under the early spring sun.

"Thanks," he said, rubbing the back of his neck. "I've actually been working on something else. A game actually—a fantasy one. Kind of a side project while I figure things out."

Belle tilted her head. "A fantasy game?"

"Women with swords," he said, grinning. "They save the world while all the guys argue about supply chains or the angle of attack."

Belle laughed, surprised. "I'd play that."

Zach hesitated, then added, quieter, "I was thinking...maybe I could model the main character after you."

Belle's smile faltered. Not in offense. In surprise. She blinked once, twice. I could see the shift—the moment she realized Zach might not just admire her work ethic.

"Oh," she said softly. "You mean...like a drawing?"

"Yeah," he said quickly, suddenly bashful again. "If you'd sit for it. Unless that's weird."

Belle's expression softened. "It's not weird." A pause. "It's...sweet, actually. That you'd think of me. I mean, you're practically my brother with our parents dating."

Standing in the background, the three of us froze. You could've heard the spring blooms shuddering back beneath their leaves.

Lana whispered, "Oh no."

Celia pressed her hands to her face. "I can't watch this." Then she pulled her hands away. "I'm gonna go rescue my baby."

Both Lana's and my hands clamped down on her shoulders to hold her still and save her son from any further embarrassment.

Zach gave himself a shake, as though coming back from floating on high. "Right. Exactly."

The two words crashed together. He gulped and then plastered a smile back on.

"I was actually thinking of making it a sibling adventure," he went on.

"So you'd model the brother character after you?" Belle said. "Tall, handsome, and capable?"

"You think I'm capable?"

Funny how Zach latched on to that adjective rather than the one about his looks. And just like that, his chest puffed up again.

Celia covered her face with both hands. "I have to stop this. Look, he's sweating through his shirt." She started to step forward, but Lana caught her wrist.

"Let the boy suffer a little. It builds character."

"He's my son, not a sourdough starter," Celia hissed.

I smiled, trying to defuse them both. "I think it's sweet."

Once upon a time, someone had looked at me the way Zach was looking at Belle. My husband had adored me, entirely and without hesitation. I'd loved him back fiercely until the end. It was when the end came that I realized that I had wanted more.

Bo Porter's laugh carried before he even reached us, warm and sure like a man who'd finally stopped fighting his own happiness. Theo Marsden trailed beside him, tall and steady, his hand already seeking out Lana's without looking.

"Ladies," Bo said, sweeping an arm around Celia's waist. "Everything looks perfect. You've outdone yourselves."

Theo kissed Lana's temple, his voice low and teasing. "Of course it does. These women built the whole Jubilee, the Holiday Market, and now the Spring Fair with just a raise of the eyebrow."

Bo grinned. "I helped. I brought the ladder."

Celia rolled her eyes but leaned into him all the same. Lana melted into Theo's side with a soft, content sigh. It was the kind of sound that didn't need an audience, just a safe place to land.

Both men greeted me with the same easy affection they always did. Bo's one-armed hug was warm and solid. Theo's shoulder squeeze was quick but sincere, his eyes kind.

And still, the warmth didn't reach the chill that lived somewhere deep in my sternum.

My friends were both building second families—messy, beautiful, noisy lives stitched back together from the scraps of loss that was divorce. They'd rebuilt with these new loves. Both their version 2.0 loves were serious upgrades.

For so long, I'd told myself I didn't want that. That dating again would be like reopening an old wound. That I had enough—my yoga studio, my students, my peace.

But watching them now—hands entwined, laughter shared so easily—I could no longer deny the truth: There was something else I wanted. Something my husband had refused to give me. Something that didn't require falling in love.

I wanted to nurture again. And for the first time, I wasn't ashamed of it.

So later that afternoon, while the bunting fluttered and the town hummed with celebration, I took a breath that wasn't practiced or measured. It was shaky. Then I drove to the adoption agency. Because peace had kept me still long enough. It was time to move.

CHAPTER TWO

I sat on the edge of the chair across from a desk that was too big for the room. My hands were folded neatly in my lap like a student waiting for permission to speak. The adoption agency was two towns over by design. I loved Stillwater, but privacy was as rare there as a quiet booth at Suny's Diner.

Old Man Wendall would've seen me walk through any door in town and made a full report while pretending to read the newspaper over his morning coffee. Rita, the waitress at Suny's, could spread gossip faster than she poured a dark brew over the lunchtime rush—always with a smile and a refill. And Ms. Thelma? She'd clutch her pearls, whisper every detail across the church pews during evening service, and call it fellowship.

I wasn't ready to be that conversation piece. So here I was, two towns over, heart hammering like a teenager about to confess something reckless, hoping the quiet outside Stillwater's borders would give me room to breathe long enough to say the thing I'd been carrying for years.

I wanted to be a mother.

Even now. Even at my age. Even after agreeing once upon a time that it wasn't in the cards for me.

And I didn't want the whole town watching me try to claim that dream before I even had the chance.

The adoption agent, a woman with silver hair threaded through her raven locks, glanced up from her computer. Her expression wasn't unkind exactly. Just...tired.

"So," she said, drawing out the word like she was pulling taffy. "You're forty-seven."

I smiled, serene. "Yes."

"And you'd like to adopt a baby."

"I would."

She tilted her head, pen tapping against her notepad. The placard on her desk read Janice Harlow. "A newborn?"

"If possible."

Janice's tapping stopped. Her eyes lifted to meet mine, one brow arched with that particular brand of bureaucratic skepticism. "You know, Ms. Bloom, most women of your advanced age are thinking about grandchildren, not midnight feedings."

I breathed in. Counted to four. Exhaled slowly, evenly. *Advanced age.* I offered her the practiced smile I used when a student complained that meditation was boring.

"Men have babies well into their eighties, don't they? And women are usually the ones who end up caring for them."

Janice gave a short laugh. It was more an exhale than a sound. "Fair point."

Encouraged, I leaned in slightly. "I'm not trying to get pregnant. I'm aware of biology and…its sense of humor. There are so many new souls who need love and stability. I have both. I'd like to share them."

The words came out smooth, but the memory they stirred caught in my throat like dust. I was nineteen again, sitting on a splintered bench under a magnolia tree at the university quad, my knees pressed against Darnell's.

He was city-born, the kind of man who carried the hum of traffic in his heartbeat and always smelled faintly of rain and exhaust fumes. The first time I met him, he'd offered me his last pen during an exam. The second time, he'd offered me half his sandwich. By the third, I was already sure: *He's it.*

He was kind the way some people are naturally musical—instinctive, effortless. He called his mother every Sunday, showed up for every friend who needed help moving, remembered the names of janitors and bus drivers. I thought, *This is the man I want raising my children.*

Months passed, and our relationship had gotten serious. I could see it on the horizon. The question hung in the air: Where is this relationship going? But I was already certain of its trajectory. Then one afternoon, in that same spot under the magnolia tree, he took my hand and changed the shape of my future.

"I don't want kids, Tess."

He said it gently, the way you'd tell someone you couldn't make it to dinner after all. No cruelty, just quiet conviction.

The world tilted, just a fraction. The sunlight that had been so soft on his face seemed suddenly too bright.

"Oh," I'd said because there was no script for that kind of moment.

Darnell squeezed my hand. "I just... I can't risk

passing this on. My mother's sickle cell, the disease that took her life, it's in my blood. I can't ask anyone to live through that."

He looked so certain, so good, so heartbreakingly good. I should have walked away. I knew that. But love makes strange mathematicians of us all. It teaches us to subtract what we want most just to keep the equation balanced.

So I'd smiled, serene even then. "That's all right," I'd told him. "I don't need children. All I need is you."

He'd kissed my forehead in relief, and that was the moment I fell the rest of the way in love with him.

It hadn't been a lie. Not at the time. But thirty years later in a life without him, it had caught up to me.

I never regretted it. Not then. Not when we moved back to Stillwater and built a life full of soft mornings and quiet laughter. Not even when I held his hand through the nights that hurt him most, when that asshole of a disease had come for his body.

Sickle cell had a way of pretending to sleep before it sinks its teeth in. Some nights it was the pain crises that bent him double, heat packs lining his spine like makeshift armor. Other times it was the bone-deep fatigue, the feeling that his blood was moving through him like gravel instead of life. There were hospital stays, transfusions, the careful monitoring of hydration and temperature, and every small trigger that could send him spiraling.

I stayed beside him through all of it. Because I had loved that man long before I knew the word crisis meant something entirely different for him than it did for most people.

Only now, sitting across from Mrs. Harlow and her skeptical pen, did the regret come whispering through—small, insistent, like a child pressing her face against a window, asking to be let in.

Janice just looked at me, her pen stilled. I felt the energy between us shift. Her weariness collided with my calm until something softer settled in the air.

That's always been my gift. I can make people breathe easy. It's not much of a superpower. I don't expect the Avengers to be banging down my door because I am good at deescalating and not blowing up buildings. I can talk anyone down from their cliff with a gentle tone and steady eye contact. It's not manipulation—it's empathy, refined into muscle memory.

"Tell me about your home," Mrs. Harlow said finally, her voice less clipped.

So I did. I told her about the sunlight in my kitchen, the smell of lavender oil that lingered in the walls, and the extra bedrooms. I told her about Stillwater, the town that never quite moved on but always managed to heal itself in small, stubborn ways.

"How does your husband feel about this? I'll need both of you here for the paperwork."

"It's just me." I rolled the gold band around on my left hand. I had never considered taking it off all these years later. In my mind, in my heart, I was still very much married. "My husband is no longer with us."

Mrs. Harlow nodded as if all of it made sense now. "What made you decide you wanted to adopt now?"

The question was simple. My pulse beat a complicated rhythm.

I drew a breath so deep it reached the places I usually avoid. "My husband had sickle cell. He was terrified of passing it on. I told him I didn't mind, that I didn't need children to feel whole. And for a long time, that was true. We had a good life. Now that he's gone, I think the part of me that used to want a child woke up again. I kept it buried for so long I forgot it was still breathing."

Mrs. Harlow typed something into her computer. "You understand that newborns are in high demand," she said without looking at me. "Hard to come by."

"I understand."

"Have you ever been to a kennel?"

I blinked. "A kennel?"

She glanced up, a little apologetic. "Puppies and kittens are always the first to go."

"I know this won't be immediate. Patience is my strongest virtue."

She stared at me for a moment, then something eased in her shoulders. "I'll see what we can do."

As she typed, I watched the cursor blink on the screen—steady, rhythmic, like a heartbeat. Peace, I reminded myself, isn't the absence of wanting. It's the courage to want, anyway.

CHAPTER THREE

The scent of sandalwood lingered in the air, even after the last namaste had faded. Afternoon light slanted through the studio's windows in long, honey-colored ribbons, catching in the soft haze of incense smoke. The room felt balanced: bodies and breath now gone, peace left behind like a faint echo.

"Keep your breaths soft," I'd told them at the start of class. "Let it be a quiet conversation between your body and your soul."

They'd listened. Or at least, they'd tried. I moved between them with a practiced grace, my voice low and fluid. A pregnant student near the window— sweet Naomi, six months along and determined—

tried to ease herself into half-moon pose. Her ankle wobbled; her balance faltered.

"Breathe," I said gently, stepping closer. "Find the ground before you rise."

She smiled, flustered, cheeks pink with effort. I steadied her hand lightly, but inside, my chest tightened. Just for a breath. Just long enough for something sharp to slip through the calm.

I'd learned not to let that flicker show. Grief was an old visitor, polite enough to knock before entering. I exhaled and smoothed my voice back to silk. "There you go. Beautiful."

When the final class bell chimed and the room dimmed, bodies melted into Savasana. I moved through the rows like a whisper, adjusting a shoulder here, brushing a palm across a brow there. My students drifted. Their breaths slowed. One by one, they returned from the edge of themselves, then got up one vertebra at a time and rolled their mats.

Except one.

A new student—tall, blond streaks in her hair, her mat still perfectly unrolled—had fallen asleep. Her chest rose and fell in a deep, unguarded rhythm, her arms loose at her sides.

I almost woke her. Almost. Something about her

surrender—the rare kind that comes only when someone's been holding too much for too long—made me let her rest.

The others trickled out, their laughter fading into the hallway. I tidied up blocks and blankets, pretending not to notice the gentle snore from the corner from my snoozing student.

Then her phone rang. Or rather, it screamed. A guttural woman sing-screaming at the top of her lungs about how much she hated her ex, followed by another visceral scream. It took my mind a few seconds to place the song "Caught Out There" by Kelis. The raw, female fury about a bad breakup that had blared across the R&B stations in the late '90s. That was this woman's ringtone?

The blond ex-hater jolted awake with a gasp. "Damn it. Why can't you just let me rest in peace!"

Her hair was askew, her yoga top twisted. When her eyes found me, mortification flickered across her face. Just like the switch between Kelis' screaming chorus and the dulcet verses, the blond's voice changed. "Oh my God, I'm so sorry. I didn't mean to—did everyone already leave?"

I smiled softly. "They did. You looked like you needed the rest."

She huffed a laugh that didn't reach her eyes. "I

guess I did." The phone buzzed again or rather screamed. She grabbed it from her bag, scowling at the screen. "Of course, it's him again."

I said nothing, merely folded a towel and placed it on the stack. The rhythm of movement steadied me.

"It's my ex-husband," she said, more to herself than to me. "We share custody of the kids. He's supposed to drop them off to me at my place, but now he's panicking because I'm not there yet. Like, I can't take one hour for myself without someone losing their mind."

Her thumbs flew over the screen. The sound of her tapping filled the room, sharp and rhythmic like a woodpecker going at a tree that couldn't get out of its way.

"'I told you I'd be late,'" she muttered aloud, reading as she typed. "'You'll survive an extra thirty minutes of parenting.' God, he acts like I'm abandoning ship."

I busied myself with the incense tray, giving her space to unravel.

She sighed heavily, dropped the phone back into her bag, then looked up at me as if expecting a witness, or maybe an ally. "You know what I mean, right? Men. They always think we're the ones who can't handle a crisis, but hand them a baby in need of a diaper change and they crumble."

Her tone teetered between anger and exhaustion. Beneath it, I heard the tremor I recognized in so many women. It was the one that hides under *I'm fine.*

I met her gaze, smiled in that slow, measured way that had gotten me through funerals, tantrums, and town board meetings alike. "Parenting is a kind of yoga, I think. Everyone trying to find their balance, no one quite nailing the pose."

"Yeah, well, if parenting's yoga, I'm permanently stuck in downward cow." Her laugh came out brittle, like she was trying to make herself believe it was funny.

"Dog," I corrected.

"Beg pardon?"

"It's downward dog."

She reached into her bag for her keys but didn't move to stand. "Sorry. Long day. I'm a social worker over at the county. My name's Marianne, by the way. Sometimes I think I collect other people's disasters for a living."

I tilted my head. "That sounds like important work."

"It's work." Marianne's tone was flat. But then her

face softened. "I love my job. I love my kids. But sometimes…" She let out a breath, the kind that sounded like it had been trapped in her chest for years. "Sometimes I wish I could just have a day where nobody needed saving."

I brushed incense ashes into a trash can, waiting. People often tell you the truth when you let silence make space for it. I picked up a weighted blanket and began to fold it.

Marianne rubbed her temples. "Like today. There's this teen—seventeen years old and pregnant. She was hiding it from her parents. They found out and kicked her out." Her voice hardened, protective and weary all at once. "Now I'm supposed to find her housing before the end of the week. A scared kid with nowhere to go and a baby on the way. And she doesn't even want the kid."

I froze mid-fold. The lavender scent from the blanket drifted up, sweet and aching.

Marianne didn't notice. She was staring down at her phone again, thumb hovering, jaw tight. "Sorry. You didn't sign up for a therapy session. I just needed to vent."

"It's all right," I said quietly, keeping my tone even though my pulse had begun a soft, steady drum. "Sometimes talking is its own kind of rest."

Marianne smiled, tired but genuine this time. "Guess I should come to your class more often."

"I hope you do."

She stood to leave. I watched her go. At the last possible second, I chased her out the door.

CHAPTER FOUR

The café was crowded in that cozy Stillwater way. Bean There was filled with mismatched mugs and old wood tables polished smooth by gossip and years. The air smelled like roasted beans and cinnamon scones, the kind of scent that could make anyone believe in second chances.

Lana and Celia were in rare form this morning, perched across from me like a mismatched pair of talk-show hosts. I smiled when they laughed, nodded at the right intervals, and stirred my tea more times than necessary. My spoon clinked gently against the cup, the steady rhythm of someone pretending she wasn't checking the clock every three minutes.

"Can you believe it?" Celia said, leaning in. "Zach didn't even care he didn't get that job at the design firm. He said something about 'creative freedom' like exposure pays the electric bill. Meanwhile, he keeps offering to do free work for Belle."

Lana made a sound somewhere between sympathy and mockery. "At least he's doing something. Chloe's still off backpacking through Indonesia, 'finding herself.'" She made air quotes of exasperation. "And Emily just moved in with my mother because apparently I'm too controlling."

"Maybe she just needed space," I offered softly.

Lana shot me a look that suggested space was an alien concept. "She's twenty-two, Tessa. She can have space in her own apartment."

I peered into my cup; the tea was cooling faster than I could drink it.

They went on—Celia wringing her hands about Zach's unpaid art projects for Belle Porter, Lana lamenting that at least one of her kids had a steady paycheck. I let their conversation wash over me like background music as my thoughts drifted.

If I'd had children when they did, I wondered, would I have done it differently?

I liked to think I would have. I would have given them the freedom to breathe, to stumble, to figure out who they were without mistaking rebellion for disrespect. I would have let them fail, and then helped them try again.

I admired Chloe, truth be told. There was something brave about not knowing who you were and deciding to go find out anyway. Halfway across the world without any backup. All she asked of her mother was to house her stuff while she traveled.

Emily—and Zach, for that matter—still needed the kind of gentle steering that didn't push, just guided. In some cultures, children stayed with their parents their whole lives. Then, when the time came, they cared for those parents in return. That kind of circle made sense to me.

I looked at Lana and Celia. They were both beautiful, both worn thin by years of giving everything—and wondered, not unkindly, who would take care of them when they stopped being able to take care of everyone else.

"Earth to Tessa." Lana snapped her fingers near my cup.

I blinked and looked up. "Sorry?"

"You've been staring out the window for five solid minutes," Celia said. "Who's got your attention? The hot dad?"

"The what?"

They both nodded toward the street. A man was lifting a child from the back of an SUV. The sun caught in his dark hair like it was determined to make him look softer than he clearly felt. He wore a tweed jacket—tweed, in spring—which should've seemed ridiculous, but on him only added to the quiet, professorial charm.

Hot dad indeed.

His features were unmistakably Asian, fine-boned and elegant, with that delicate uptilt at the corner of his eyes that made him look thoughtful even when he was clearly exhausted as he wrangled the flailing child. His expression was fixed in a stern, I-am-barely-holding-this-together line I knew all too well from watching my siblings and my best friends' parent over the years.

"I wasn't looking at him." Though I was still, in fact, looking at him as I sipped my tea. "You know I'm not interested in dating."

Lana grinned. "You don't have to go out with him, Tess. You could always stay in with him."

Celia snorted into her coffee. "God, Lana."

Before I could roll my eyes, the hot dad's little girl decided to stage a protest on the sidewalk. She flung a stuffed rabbit, kicking tiny sneakers against the curb. The man froze mid-reach, helpless in the way only a parent facing a public tantrum can be. But he didn't stay helpless. His handsome face went emotionless. I couldn't hear him, but the way his lips moved and his finger wagged spoke volumes as he chastised one kid, while another slightly older little boy looked close to tears as he looked on.

"Oh dear," Celia murmured.

If it had been my child, I would've knelt down. Lowered myself to eye level, spoke softly, validated the storm until it passed. Children needed to feel seen, not subdued.

A strange thought stirred then—warm and electric, equal parts hope and fear. *If it was my child.*

It might be soon. I was going to have a child of my own. Sooner than the adoption agency would allow me to. Because I wasn't going to the kennel to pick up a kitten any longer.

I checked my watch again.

"I should get going," I said, setting my cup aside and standing. "I have an appointment."

"Where are you rushing off to? You don't have any classes until later this afternoon," Lana called after me. But I didn't answer.

I stepped out into the crisp air. My heart was beating just a little too fast for someone who claimed to have made peace her full-time job. The door closed behind me; the bell chimed. It was a soft, pleasant sound that couldn't quite drown out the sharper one beyond it.

"Enough, Ellie. I said no."

The hot dad's voice cut through the chatter of Main Street. Not loud exactly but clipped—like a door slamming on patience. The little girl's wails caught mid-breath, her face blotchy and trembling.

Hot dad crouched then, one hand still gripping the discarded stuffed animal, the other resting gently on the child's arm. "You can be upset. But you still have to hold my hand to cross the street. That's not up for debate."

The child hiccupped, clutching at the stuffed rabbit he handed to her, and finally obeyed.

My throat tightened. There was no tenderness in his tone. No softness to cushion the lesson. Just command. Control.

The dad stood, slinging a brown leather satchel over his shoulder. The sharp set of his shoulders told me all I needed to know: another parent snapping under pressure, confusing authority for love.

When his eyes flicked up and met mine across the parking lot, something like embarrassment—or maybe defensiveness—passed over his face. He gave a curt nod before rounding the car and shutting the door a little too firmly.

I looked away first. Smoothing my skirt, I tried to shake the echo of his clipped tone from my ears. A quiet thrill threaded beneath my ribs. If things went well today, I would have the chance to do it differently—to soothe instead of scold, to guide instead of command.

Time to meet Marianne.

Time to see if my hard-earned peace could be shared with the unborn child of a pregnant, runaway teen.

CHAPTER FIVE

I'd parked two blocks away, half-hoping the walk would clear my nerves. It didn't.

I'd lived here all my life, but I'd never been to this particular building. The Child Protective Services building sat at the corner of Main and Willow like a stubborn relic—square, sun-faded, and patched over from decades of fairs, flu-shot clinics, bingo nights, and school board brawls. A slightly crooked banner for the Spring Fair fluttered above the door, its edges curling from having survived the Fall Jubilee and the Christmas Market before that. Inside I was met with tired carpet, posters curling at the edges, the air thick with the hum of computers and too many stories left unresolved.

Marianne met me in the lobby with a quick wave. "You found it," she said, her smile genuine if a little worn around the edges.

"Eventually," I said. "My GPS tried to send me to a bail bonds place first."

I'd never been to the bond place either. I hadn't ever had the need. I was from a happy home with two stable parents and siblings who behaved and got along. My marriage had been a happy one. My neighbors and their children never caused any ruckus, so CPS was never called, and I'd never had to post bail. Not even during Lana's dark times before her divorce. I didn't even know the number to call this place.

"That tracks," Marianne said with a sigh, gesturing me toward the hallway. "We're next door to Probation. It's good for perspective."

As we walked, she waved to coworkers who offered quick smiles—or worse, no acknowledgment at all. One woman barely lifted her head from her keyboard. A man in a rumpled shirt gave Marianne a polite nod, then rolled his eyes the moment her back was turned.

"This place," Marianne muttered under her breath. "It'll either make you a saint or a cynic."

Her office was small but lived-in: overstuffed file

folders stacked like leaning towers, a mug of cold coffee on the desk, a few crayon drawings taped to the wall.

She motioned for me to sit, then settled behind her desk, rubbing her temple. "Okay, let's get right to it. The girl's name is Lila. Seventeen. Pregnant. Parents kicked her out when they found out."

I clasped my hands in my lap, keeping my breathing slow, deliberate. "You haven't found her a foster home yet?"

Marianne shook her head. "Not one that'll take a pregnant teen. Everyone's full, or they don't want the liability." She sighed, flipping through a thin folder. "She's at the hospital now, getting checked out. But she can't stay there much longer."

I didn't think. I just spoke. "She can come stay with me. I have plenty of space. And I want to help."

Marianne's eyes softened, but her mouth didn't follow. "I know you do. But let's be clear; you have an ulterior motive, remember? You want to adopt her baby."

I blinked, feeling my composure falter. "Is that… illegal?"

"No," Marianne said carefully. "But it can look… ethically hairy. If someone wants to make it messy, they could."

Her words made me shrink back slightly in the chair. The office suddenly felt smaller, the walls too close.

Marianne's expression softened. "Hey," she said, reaching across the desk to touch my hand. "I'm on your side. I think you'd make an excellent mother with all that Zen in your bones. Truth be told, I don't understand why you'd want to be one. Your life looks pretty good as is."

I frowned, unsure if it was an insult or an observation. I looked again at the crayon-colored pictures on her walls. I knew she had kids because she had an ex-husband who had wanted to drop them off to her. I surmised that her relationship with her ex was contentious. But was it the same with her children? If it was, this was an odd job to have—working for the protection of other people's children.

Marianne reached into a drawer and pulled out a form, sliding it toward me. "This is an emergency caregiver application. You fill that out, and I'll talk to my supervisor about clearing you to meet Lila."

"I can do that."

Marianne nodded, stood, and grabbed her coffee mug. "I'll be right back. Don't go anywhere."

The door clicked shut behind her, leaving only the sound of a humming vent and my own heartbeat.

I picked up the pen, the cheap plastic kind that always leaks, and started writing despite the pen skipping every other letter.

Name: Tessa Bloom.

Occupation: Yoga instructor.

Marital status: Widow.

I stared at the word *widow*. It looked strange on paper—too small for everything it contained. I dotted the "i" over the word a little too hard, leaving a tiny blot of ink. That's when I heard the knock.

It was firm, masculine. Before I could answer that Marianne wasn't here, the door opened halfway.

"MJ, you can't pull a stunt like you did the other day. Ellie was—"

I knew that voice. I'd only heard it once—sharp and commanding, cutting through the morning air like a reprimand—but it had lived rent-free in my head since the coffee shop.

When I looked up, there he was.

Hot Dad.

He stood in the doorway, tall and solid, wearing that tweed jacket and the faint look of a man who'd been running on fumes. Up close, he was... more. More handsome, more solid, more hot.

The tweed jacket I'd noticed earlier looked even more professorial under fluorescent lighting—

textured, warm, a little rumpled. His tie was unexpectedly sleek and slate-colored, the kind of tie that made my mind skip—briefly, embarrassingly—to a certain trilogy of books I'd pretended not to enjoy while throwing shade to the friends who liked the books and the movie.

His dark eyes were ringed with the soft lines of someone who smiled often, even if he wasn't doing it now. The faint crow's-feet gave him away. Smile lines on a man were dangerous; they could make a woman imagine being the person who put them there.

And then there were his legs—long, lean, the kind that made me swallow before I could stop myself. It startled me the way my body reacted to him. I hadn't felt that thrum—sharp, unbidden, alive—since the first time I'd laid eyes on Darnell across a freshman-year Intro to Psychology class, both of us pretending not to stare.

Hot Dad's eyes widened a fraction when he recognized me, like he'd forgotten I existed until I was suddenly there. Then he smoothed it away with the practiced composure of a man who lived a careful life.

"Oh," he said, lowering his hand from the doorframe. "I'm sorry. I thought you were my ex-wife."

He was leaning against the doorframe. Not just standing—leaning. It hit me all at once: Jordan Catalano.

When I was a teenager, my friends swooned over rock stars and football players. I had *My So-Called Life*. And Jordan Catalano—brooding, unreachable— always leaned. Against lockers, against cars, against the idea of being understood. I used to think that posture meant confidence. Now I recognized it for what it was: exhaustion disguised as cool.

This man—Marianne's ex-husband, I realized with a small jolt—was doing the same thing. One shoulder braced against the frame, hands in his pockets, like Atlas casually holding up a world that didn't deserve his broad shoulders. And they were broad. My God, were they broad.

He gave a short, awkward laugh that didn't quite reach his eyes, then stayed exactly where he was— still leaning, still holding up invisible weight—while I tried not to stare too long at the curve of his jaw or the shadow of something tired in his expression.

Before I could find something graceful to say, Marianne's voice rang from the hall. "Hiro? What are you doing in my office?"

That just wasn't fair. The man leaned like my teenage crush, and he was named Hiro.

CHAPTER SIX

The chairs outside Marianne's office were the color of old oatmeal: stitched vinyl that squeaked when you shifted and left the faint smell of antiseptic on your clothes. I sat perched on one, knees together, hands folded neatly in my lap, trying not to breathe too deeply. The air in Child Protective Services was thick with other people's stories.

Not the sweet kind. Not the ones told over kitchen tables with warm bread and laughter. No, these were the stories that seeped into the drywall and the vents, lingering even after the families who'd carried them had walked out.

Tears had a scent here—salt and something metallic, like hope rubbed raw.

Anger had one too, sharp and acrid, like over-heated wires behind a wall.

And anguish—even worse. It clung low and damp, like the moment before a storm breaks, when the air tastes of regret and you can't tell if the heaviness is in the clouds or in your own chest.

Every breath I took felt like borrowing someone else's hurt. So I sat very still, spine straight, breathing shallowly through my nose like I could keep the ache at a polite distance. But the stories lived in the carpet, in the squeaking vinyl, in the recycled air. They settled over me anyway, quiet and stubborn as dust.

Behind the closed door, voices rose.

Actually—one voice rose.

Marianne's.

"Do you ever think about how this looks?" she snapped, words sharp enough to cut through the thin walls.

Then came the low rumble of a man's reply—steady, contained. That voice. Even muted, it sounded the same as it had in the parking lot: calm, patient, maddeningly measured. I couldn't make out the words, but I recognized the tone. The tone of a man who could hold his temper like a stone in his palm and make it look like peace.

I glanced around. The receptionist didn't even flinch. A man with a file tucked under his arm sighed. Someone else clicked a pen, unimpressed. Apparently, this was routine.

I shifted in my seat. Darnell and I had disagreed sometimes—about bills, about my mother's visits, about whether we could handle another round of hospital stays—but never like this. Never in public, and never long enough that anyone else could hear.

The door rattled once, as if Marianne had slammed a hand against her desk. "You can't just decide things for both of us, Hiro!"

The low voice answered again, too soft to make out, which somehow made it worse.

I took a slow breath in through my nose and out through my mouth. Tried to focus on the smell of lavender oil clinging to my sleeve instead of the tension humming behind the door.

The chime over the front of the door sounded. I looked up.

A girl stood in the hallway—no, not a girl. A young woman. Barely.

She couldn't have been more than seventeen. Her belly jutted out beneath an oversized hoodie, round and precarious. Her skin was pale enough to show freckles. Her red hair was pulled into a messy braid that frayed around her face. She was too thin every-where except where she wasn't. It was like her body had spent everything it had to grow the little person sharing her being.

Her eyes darted to the closed door. When Mari-anne's voice spiked again, the girl's shoulders jumped.

"Is, um…" she started, then stopped, glancing toward the receptionist's desk. Her voice was small, careful. "Is Ms. Marianne in there?"

I rose before I could think. "She is," I said gently. "But she's a little busy at the moment."

The girl nodded, eyes wide and uncertain.

"Are you waiting to see her?" I asked, though I already knew.

Another nod.

I smiled, soft and practiced. "Then you must be Lila."

Her surprise flickered across her face like a candle flame. "How'd you know?"

I held up the paperwork I'd finished a few minutes ago. "I'm filling out paperwork to be your emergency shelter. I'm Tessa." I gestured to the empty chair beside mine. "Would you like to sit?"

Lila hesitated. She shifted her weight awkwardly before lowering herself down with a small grunt. Her hands rested protectively on her belly, fingers tapping an anxious rhythm.

For a moment, we just sat in the stale hallway air, listening to Marianne's muffled frustration and the answering murmur of Hiro's calm.

Lila blew a strand of hair from her face. "Parents fight a lot," she said quietly.

I wasn't sure if she meant the voices behind the door, her own parents, or adults in general.

"Sometimes people who care about the same thing just... care differently," I offered. "It doesn't mean they don't want the same outcome."

Lila looked at me sidelong, skeptical but not dismissive. "My parents don't want to be grandparents. At least not without me having a ring on my finger."

"The baby's father isn't in the picture?"

Lila shook her head, eyes on her shoes.

We fell into silence again, the kind that wasn't comfortable but wasn't entirely awkward either. Just... waiting.

Finally, I said, "Would you like me to wait with you? Until she's done?"

Lila shrugged one shoulder but didn't say no. Her

fingers kept moving over her belly, tracing invisible circles, soothing someone—or maybe herself. Her belly grumbled.

"Want to go and grab a bite to eat?"

She looked up at me. Then she nodded.

CHAPTER SEVEN

Suny's Diner was the color of strawberry milk: pink walls, pink booths, even a faded pink clock above the counter that had given up keeping time sometime during the Reagan administration. The place had opened after the First World War, and I was fairly sure the waitress had been there ever since.

Her name tag said Rita, though she didn't need it. Everyone in Stillwater knew Rita. She had a curly mop of hair that defied gravity and common sense, and her coffee pot might as well have been surgically attached to her hand. She reminded me of the waitress from Mel's Diner, the one who called everyone "Hun," but with a slightly sharper edge—like she'd call you "Hun" and then tell your mama what you were up to.

Lila and I sat in a booth near the window, sunlight slanting through the blinds in thin, forgiving stripes. The teen mom looked around the diner like she wasn't sure whether to sit taller or slouch so she might disappear entirely. I felt her nervous energy like static clinging to a sweater just out of the drier.

Rita appeared, coffee pot poised, eyes squinting between us. "What'll it be, honey?"

Lila glanced at the menu, then at Rita, then down at her lap. "Just toast."

Rita's brows rose. "Just toast?"

Lila nodded, fiddling with her napkin. She kept her eyes on her water glass like the bubbles in the ice might tell her what she was allowed to want.

My heart ached. I'd seen that look before—in kids who learned early that wanting meant trouble. Rita saw it too; her mouth pressed into a thin line. Rita looked at me, suspicion written in every line of her face. In a town like Stillwater, an older woman having lunch with a pregnant teenager was the kind of thing that set the grapevine vibrating by dessert.

"I'll have the lasagna special," I said. "And a side of vegetables, please. It's my first time ordering it here.

My husband was allergic to dairy, so I've always wanted to try it."

That earned a pause—just long enough for Rita's expression to soften a hair. I knew that look. It was the look of a poor-pitiful-widow look. I hated that look.

"How you holding up, hun?" she asked. "You eating enough? Sleeping at all?"

Rita's features softened further in that unmistakable way they always did when Darnell's name hovered between me and someone who knew him. It was like she could still see him walking through the door, smiling kindly at everyone, even on the days the pain sat behind his eyes.

"I'm doing fine, Ms. Rita, thank you."

Rita's gaze gentled even more. "I'm sure your beloved husband is fussing at you from heaven for not eating my lasagna until now."

Before she turned to leave, she brightened suddenly—as though remembering her civic duty as Stillwater's unofficial matchmaker. "You know, my son's single again. Third wife ran off, bless her heart. He's a little bruised up but a hard worker. Good with his hands. I could send him your way if you're looking."

I managed not to choke on my own breath.

Barely. "I'm sure another woman will snap him right up."

Rita arched a brow. "Could be you."

I gulped, the way you do right before stepping into cold water, and pasted on a serene little smile—the one I used when I needed to seem calmer than I felt.

"We'll let the universe decide."

Rita snorted, but her hand brushed my shoulder as she passed. "Lasagna, veggies, one toast. Be out in a bit, hun."

When she left, I exhaled quietly. The hum of conversation around us returned—spoons clinking, laughter at the counter, the low hiss of the griddle.

"Tell me about yourself, Lila."

Her eyes darted up, then down again. "About me?"

"Yes," I said, gently but insistently. "Where you're from, what you like to do—anything."

She shifted, pressing a palm against the table's sticky vinyl edge. "There's not much to tell."

"Which high school did you go to?" There were only two in Stillwater. One public school and one private school.

"I was homeschooled. I got my GED last year."

Homeschooling wasn't unheard of here.

Although most parents in Stillwater wanted their kids to have a crowd to cheer with on Friday nights or a bake sale to complain about rather than keep it all inside the home.

"What was your favorite subject?"

"Math," she said immediately, then added, "I liked that there was always a right answer. You didn't have to guess what someone wanted. With history or English, it was hard to figure out what my mom wanted me to say in an essay or oral report." The words slipped out like she hadn't meant them to. Her lips pressed together as soon as they were free, her hand moving protectively to her belly.

I didn't press. Instead, I smiled softly and said, "I liked everything at school. I was one of those students who thought extra credit was a surprise gift. When I went to college, I was so unfocused that I wound up graduating with an M.R.S."

Lila frowned. "What's that?"

"It means I found a husband instead of a career. My mother was thrilled. I'd told her I wasn't going to be the kind of woman who married young, but then I met Darnell." Saying his name still caught on my tongue, like a bead snagging a thread. "We built a life together. I stayed home while he worked, and then, when he couldn't work anymore…" My voice softened to a thread. "I took care of him."

Lila was watching me, careful and uncertain. Pity, maybe, or discomfort. I couldn't blame her. Grief makes people flinch, even secondhand.

"I met the baby's father in college," she said after a long pause. Her voice was tentative, like stepping onto thin ice. "I registered for a math class—trig. My mom couldn't teach it to me. That's where I met him."

I nodded slowly. "Does he… want to be involved?"

She shook her head, eyes fixed on the table. "He doesn't believe it's his. Says we were never even together."

Something inside me folded in on itself. The instinct to soothe—to fix—rose like breath. Without thinking, I reached across the table. My palm rested open, a quiet invitation.

Lila startled, her eyes flicking to my hand, then back to my face. Her shoulders tensed, and I wondered how long it had been since someone had reached for her without demanding something in return.

Before she could decide what to do, Rita appeared, balancing two steaming plates.

"Lasagna special," she said, sliding the dish in front of me, "and toast."

"Thank you," I said smoothly, my hand withdrawing as I reached for the silverware.

Rita lingered a beat too long before shuffling off, muttering something about refilling coffee cups.

I pushed the lasagna toward the middle of the table, the scent of garlic and tomato sauce softening the moment.

"You don't have to, you know," Lila said, still not meeting my eyes.

"Have to what?"

"Be nice to me. I know you just want the baby."

I let out a slow breath, the kind that smoothed edges before words slipped through. "I do want to be a mother to your baby. But that doesn't mean I can't get to know you, too. I figure it's reconnaissance for when the baby is older."

Lila frowned. "Reconnaissance?"

"If the child comes to me one day wanting to take advanced trigonometry, I'll already know which tutor to call—because Lord knows I won't have any of the answers."

That drew a small, genuine laugh from the teen mom—bright and unguarded. "You'd get the baby a tutor?"

"Of course." I set my fork down; the clink was small but certain. "I think children are little people with big souls. They just don't know how to manage them yet. It's our job to guide them through the noise, not control the melody. Parents shouldn't bend their children into shape. They should help them unfold into who they already are."

Lila's expression softened, some shadow lifting from her features. She nodded, reaching for her fork, and took a helping of lasagna.

CHAPTER EIGHT

The sun hung low over Stillwater's grocery store, turning the parking lot asphalt to something almost soft. It was like the heat had melted all the edges off the day. I spotted Zach leaning against the cart return, hands tucked into his pockets, his hair catching the light the way Celia's used to when we were young and too sure of everything.

"Hey, Zach Attack."

He frowned at the name but didn't ask for any clarification. I swore I heard the *Okay, Boomer* in the raise of his brows. Since he didn't call me a Boomer out loud, I couldn't correct him about my generation.

"Hey, Miss Tessa."

"You look like a man on a mission."

Zach's features relaxed into that lopsided grin I remembered from the days he trailed after us at barbecues, all scraped knees and stubborn charm. "I'm just waiting for Belle. She ran in to grab something for dinner."

I raised a brow. "Dinner, hm? Sounds like a date night."

Color rushed up his neck. "No, no—it's not like that. We're just friends. Practically siblings, you know?"

But the words snagged on disappointment. Zach's voice softened around them, like he wanted to believe it more than he did.

I tilted my head, the way I did when one of my students tried to convince me they loved downward dog. No one loves that pose. It's just good for the body.

"Sometimes, being someone's constant is the best way to show them what they've been missing. People don't always recognize home until they've stood in the rain for a while."

Zach chewed his lip, the way Celia used to when she was holding back tears or the truth.

I touched his arm, a brief squeeze of reassurance. "You're doing right by her, Zach. Just keep showing up. The rest will come when she's ready to see it."

He nodded, eyes thoughtful, gaze sliding toward the store's automatic doors as they opened with their usual sigh. "Thanks, Miss Tessa."

"It's Aunt Tessa."

"Yes, ma'am. I mean Aunt."

Inside the grocery store, I found Belle near the refrigerated section, inspecting a head of butter lettuce like it might confess secrets if she stared long enough.

"Hey, Belle," I said, and she turned, her face lighting up with a smile that could have powered the entire town. "Still saving Stillwater one square foot at a time?"

She laughed, brushing her hair from her face. "Trying. I'm just picking up a few things for dinner."

"For a paramour?" I asked, teasing.

Belle snorted. "No, it's just Zach and me. He helped me stage a house today, so I promised to feed him. I don't have time for romance right now."

"Friendships are the best relationships," I said. "No pressure, no performance—just presence."

Before I could say more, a sharp cry echoed down the aisle. The cry was high-pitched and sudden, followed by the unmistakable sound of something clattering to the floor but not breaking. Heads turned.

Two aisles over, a little girl sat on the tile beside a toppled display of cereal boxes, her small fists balled, her face blotched with the bright red of injustice. A boy a few years older stood nearby, embarrassed and angry by proxy.

And there—steady as a pillar in the storm—stood Hiro Tanaka.

His voice was calm but firm, deep enough to carry without rising. "Ellie. Pick it up, please."

The girl wailed louder, kicking at the boxes. Hiro didn't flinch. His tone remained maddeningly even. "You can be upset," he said. "But you can't throw things."

The girl wailed, "Mommy lets me have these."

Hiro's jaw tightened for the briefest second before he exhaled through his nose, gathering the boxes one by one. "Then when you go to Mom's house you can have them, but you're at my house tonight, and we're having pancakes in the morning."

"With chocolates in them?"

"How about blueberries?"

The little girl screwed up her face. Her brother, who had been standing staunchly by, also grimaced.

"I'll make them into happy faces."

They brightened at that.

"But first, we have to clean up this mess."

Around us, the store had fallen into that polite small-town hush that comes when everyone pretends not to stare.

I felt something cold ripple through the calm I wore like armor. If it had been me, I thought, I'd kneel lower, soften my voice, coax the child back to calm instead of containing her storm. I'd let her know her feelings were valid, not put up boundaries. And I would've picked up the boxes myself. It was a big job for little hands.

Beside me, Belle sighed. "Oh boy. That's the Tanakas."

I glanced at her. "You know him?"

"He and his wife were one of my first clients when I started here in real estate. Beautiful couple, at least on the surface. Bought a place near Willow Creek, not even a year before they split. Ugly divorce. He kept the house; she's in a two-bedroom apartment now."

"That's… unfortunate."

"Mm-hm." Belle leaned her elbows on the cart, watching the scene with an almost weary familiarity. "Those poor kids. It's not the first time they've melted down in public. Last summer at the County Fair, that little one threw herself flat on the grass over a snow cone. Her mother scooped her up under one arm, both of them screaming all the way to the parking lot. The whole town saw."

I winced, imagining it. "Stillwater never forgets a spectacle."

Belle shook her head. "Nope. I feel bad for him, but… kids that loud? I'd lose my mind."

I watched Hiro then—tall, calm, unshaken as his daughter's sobs echoed down the aisle. His patience looked less like grace and more like detachment.

Belle exhaled. "See? Not even a smile. Man's made of stone."

I nodded faintly, though I wasn't sure I agreed. Peace, I reminded myself, shouldn't look like silence after a storm.

One of the cereal boxes had landed by my feet, its cartoon tiger smiling up at me like he was in on some secret. I bent to pick it up, stacking it neatly on the shelf. Another box followed, then another. The boy was already gathering them too, small hands working fast, his face pink with effort.

"Thank you," he said shyly when he noticed me helping.

"You're doing a good job," I told him softly, giving what I hoped was a reassuring smile.

He ducked his head, and for a moment, something inside me eased—like this, this small act of kindness, could balance the sharp edges left hanging in the air.

Then I straightened. And found myself looking directly into the eyes of Hiro Tanaka.

"I appreciate the help," he said evenly, voice low and unhurried. "But I had it handled."

It wasn't unkind, exactly. Just final.

I opened my mouth, some well-meaning phrase about teamwork hovering on my tongue, but the words wilted under the quiet weight of his stare.

For a heartbeat, neither of us moved. Just two strangers, locked in the hum of fluorescent light and unspoken judgment.

Then he turned, guiding his children toward the checkout, his calm trailing behind him like a cold draft.

I stood there, hands still on the box, trying to convince myself that what I'd done was kindness—not interference.

Before they were out the door, the little boy looked back at me. He offered a tentative smile and a wave. I returned it with the brightest smile I could muster, sending him all of my positive energy. I had a feeling he needed it, standing in the middle of two warring parents.

CHAPTER NINE

By the time I lit the last stick of incense, the yoga studio smelled like sandalwood, ink, and ambition. Thursday nights were for the Writing Club. It was a mismatched gathering of women who came to bend sentences instead of spines. Celia was the ringleader, perched at the front of the room in her favorite purple shawl, hair wild from what Lana called creative energy and I called Bo Porter's doing.

Celia was glowing. Her new book was, in her words, "pouring out like honey." Lana swore it was an aftereffect of good loving. None of us disagreed.

"I'm just saying," Lana was telling her, waving a stack of printed pages, "I'd kill for that kind of focus. I've been staring at the same chapter of my self-help book for three days. My inner goddess wants to write, but my outer woman keeps checking the laundry."

A murmur of laughter rolled through the group.

"I think you should share the pages you wrote tonight, Lana. I felt that part about NASA in my bones."

Lana gave Celia a tentative smile. It wasn't just a few weeks ago that the two of them had been on the outs because of words. Words flung at each other because of what Lana had written on the page and what Celia had said about those words. But now, it would seem, bygones were actually gone.

Lana rolled her shoulders, held up the pages, pushed her readers up her nose, and began to share.

"They tell us we can have it all—the career, the kids, the soul mate, the skincare routine, the Pilates class, the spotless house. And for a while, I believed them. I was determined to juggle it all with a smile, a spreadsheet, and a color-coded family calendar that looked like it was built by NASA. But here's the truth no one tells you: You can have it all, just not all at the same time. Something always wobbles when the other thing's in the air."

There were murmurs of assent around the room, including some poetic snaps of fingers.

"When your career's thriving, the laundry's a disaster. When your relationship's hot, the work deadlines start to burn. When the kids are finally in a good place, you realize you haven't been on a date with your partner in six months. We keep trying to balance an equation that was never meant to stay even."

There were a few sniffles. A lot of dropped smiles and rubbed temples.

"I think the trick isn't to make everything fit at once—it's deciding what gets your energy now and what can wait its turn. When my kids were little, they were my whole world. When they got older, I remembered that I had one of my own. When my marriage ended, I learned I didn't need to fill every silence with someone else's voice. Priorities aren't promises—they're seasons. And every season asks for a different version of us.

"So no, you can't have it all at once. But you can have what matters most when it matters most. And if you can learn to let the rest rest—the dishes, the guilt, the noise—you'll realize you already had 'it all' the whole time."

There was silence as Lana finished. Inside the silence was a lot of deep breathing. I had to remind myself that I wasn't running a Pranayama class. It was women recognizing a truth that wasn't talked about out loud. Lana's words spoken out loud cracked the seal. Suddenly, everyone had an opinion.

"My ex thought compromise meant I agreed to do twice the work while he stayed the same," Carmen, one of the school teachers in the group muttered, and the group groaned in solidarity.

One of the moms from town—Michelle, I think —said, "Honestly? It was easier being a single mother than having a man-baby to manage, too."

That earned a round of Amens.

But then quiet, steady Miranda—the one with three kids and a minivan that always smelled faintly of Play-Doh—shook her head. "I couldn't imagine doing it without my husband. We're a team. He grounds me."

And from the back, a soft voice added, "The only reason I'm sane is because of my girlfriends."

The laughter that followed was tinged with truth. I sat cross-legged on my mat, notebook open but untouched, letting the words drift around me. Motherhood, I thought, feeling the word ripple through the air like a spell. So many stories. So many ways to lose yourself inside that title. And here I was —preparing to take it on alone.

A single mother. The phrase felt both foreign and

inevitable. Still, at least I had my girlfriends. Celia and Lana might be more preoccupied with their grown children and new men, but they were my anchors. They were proof that love could remake itself in different shapes.

Lana sidled closer, resting her chin on her palm. "Can you imagine being a mom now? Between school shootings, depression, social media... I'd never sleep again."

Celia nodded solemnly. "We made it out the other side, thank God."

They high-fived over their teacups. Then both pairs of eyes turned toward me.

"Not that you have to worry about any of that," Celia said cheerfully. "You're blissfully child-free."

"Lucky you," Lana added. "No carpool lines or TikTok drama."

I opened my mouth—felt the confession trembling on my tongue—but before I could say it, my phone buzzed against my mat. "Sorry, I have to take this."

"Since when do you have a phone in your studio?" asked Lana.

I ignored her and headed to the front to take the call. "Hello?"

"Tessa, it's Marianne."

Marianne's voice was tired, the sound of a woman trying to corral the world through sheer will.

"The paperwork's crawling through the system, but I'm doing what I can to push it through," she said. "You're on track to be cleared as an emergency safe home for Lila, but it's going to take a while."

Relief loosened my shoulders. "That's wonderful. Where is she staying now?"

There was a pause. Too long.

"I… don't know."

My breath caught. "You don't know?"

Something clattered in the background, followed by a sharp, childish wail.

"Ellie!" a deep voice barked—steady, calm, but unmistakable. Marianne sighed into the receiver. "I have to go. That's my ex. He's dropping off the kids. I'll call you when I have an update."

"Wait, Marianne—"

The line had already gone dead, leaving me alone in the hallway with the faint smell of incense and the sudden echo of a child's tantrum still ringing in my ears.

I pressed the phone to my chest, breathing slowly, steadily, deliberately—as if I could exhale peace back into a world that never seemed to stop unraveling.

"What was that all about?"

I jumped at the sound of Lana's voice.

"Just a service call," I said and passed her to take my seat back in the circle.

"She was discharged this morning. That's all we can say."

I'd started my search for Lila at the hospital because it was the only place I knew to start. The nurses at the front desk were kind but all sympathetic smiles and HIPAA walls.

I thanked them because politeness was the only weapon I had left, and stepped back into the evening. The air outside was warm, heavy with honeysuckle and exhaust. Stillwater's hospital sat on the edge of town, close enough to see the hills but far enough to pretend the world beyond the lake didn't exist. I stood in the parking lot for a long moment, unsure which direction to turn.

Lila wouldn't have gone back to her parents—not

after the way her voice had cracked when she'd told me about being kicked out. She wouldn't have wandered too far, not in her condition. I could still see the way she'd rested her hands on her belly at the diner: protective, uncertain, a little lost.

No, she'd have gone somewhere she knew. Somewhere she'd once felt safe. That's when it came to me: the community college.

She'd said she'd met the baby's father there, when she took a math class her mother couldn't teach. The memory was like a tack on the floor of my mind.

I got into my car and drove. The road wound past sleepy storefronts and slow traffic lights, every turn a whispered *please let her be okay*.

The campus was small. Just a few brick buildings nestled under oak trees that had been here longer than my family. It was the kind of place that smelled faintly of chalk dust and cafeteria pizza, and it made my heart ache a little. I'd met Darnell on a campus not so different from this one. He'd been sitting on the library steps after Psych class, reading something heavy and serious while I pretended to study but mostly just watched the way his lips moved over the words. He'd looked up at me, smiled, and that was that.

I parked near the math department at the

community college. Hopping out of my car, I walked the halls, peering into open classrooms. Students sat in rows, their faces lit by computer screens and the soft boredom of youth.

I scanned the boys' faces, wondering absurdly if I'd know him, the one who had changed everything in Lila's life without having to stay for the consequences. They all looked so carefree, so certain the world would wait for them to be ready.

It struck me then how easy it was for fathers. They don't carry the weight. They don't rearrange their bones to make room for another life. They can choose to walk away.

I pressed a hand to my chest, steadying the breath that threatened to turn sharp.

Darnell wouldn't have walked away—he'd simply wanted to spare us both a pain that felt inevitable. His body had been his own quiet battlefield, and I'd agreed to his terms. I'd told myself love was enough, that I didn't need more. And it had been—until it wasn't.

I closed my eyes, breathing through the ache that still felt too alive to be a memory. Now I had a second chance. A way to fill that hollow space with something that wasn't grief or guilt. I just had to find Lila.

The hallway was quiet except for the hum of the fluorescent lights. A door creaked open somewhere behind me. I turned, half expecting—half hoping—to see her small figure in the doorway, arms wrapped protectively around that fragile promise.

But the hall was empty. Only my footsteps, echoing softly, and the quiet rhythm of my own heart telling me *keep looking*.

The sound reached me first. A baby's cry—thin, urgent, impossible to ignore—rising above the low hum of student chatter and shuffling notebooks.

I paused in the hallway, hand still on the strap of my purse.

The crying grew louder as I passed an open classroom door. Inside, a young woman sat near the front, surrounded by papers, pens, and exhaustion. A stroller was wedged awkwardly beside her desk. The students around her shifted, some rolling their eyes, some sighing in exaggerated sympathy.

The mother fumbled with a bottle, her hands shaking as she tried to guide it toward the baby's searching mouth. The little one turned away, red-faced and furious, tiny fists batting at the air.

And then I heard him. That voice. Through the slightly ajar door, I saw him. Hiro Tanaka.

He stood at the front of the room, writing lines

of code on the whiteboard with deliberate precision. His sleeves were rolled, his tie slightly loosened, the picture of composed efficiency. The students watched as he explained.

"When a network fails, our first instinct is to panic—to assume the whole system is broken. But usually, the issue comes down to one small point of failure. A misconnection. A cable unplugged. A signal not reaching where it needs to go."

His voice carried over the baby, but the wails continued as the mother grew more panicked.

Hiro turned to the class, leaning casually against the desk. "You can't fix what you don't understand. So before you react, you observe. You test the connections. You breathe."

The baby's next wail cracked through his lecture. It was high, sharp, full of distress. Heads turned. The mom rocked the stroller gently with one hand while trying to copy down the notes with the other. The crying only grew louder, echoing off the cinderblock walls.

I took a step forward before I realized what I was about to do. My own instincts were kicking in: to help, to soothe, to relieve someone else's strain. The same instinct that used to send me to Lana's house when her girls were teething and she needed to shower in peace. We called it an Hour of Power—sixty minutes where Aunt Tessa took over and Lana got to remember she was a person again and sleep. Or stare at the wall. Whatever she wanted; I didn't judge.

I didn't get beyond the threshold of the classroom door. Because Hiro was already moving. He crossed the room in those quiet, measured steps of his, not rushed, not irritated.

"You're fine," he told the mother. "She's just signaling."

The mother muttered that she'd take the baby out of the room. Hiro shook his head.

"No. You need these notes if you want to pass the certification. Here."

He held out his arms. The young woman hesitated, then placed the squirming baby against his chest. Hiro adjusted his hold with a kind of easy familiarity—one arm cradling, one hand returning to the whiteboard.

He continued lecturing, voice steady. "Sometimes, all a system needs is a stable connection," he said, gently rocking the baby as he wrote. "Stability isn't about silence. It's about consistency."

The crying faded. The baby's tiny body relaxed against his shirt. Hiro, or rather Professor Tanaka, didn't smile or make a show of it. He just kept going, steady as a heartbeat. For one dizzy, disorienting moment, I felt something that might have been admiration—or maybe envy—for how easily he could restore order to chaos with nothing but quiet control.

He looked up and caught my gaze. There was a flicker of recognition in that dark gaze of his. He raised an eyebrow as though to ask what I was doing here.

I backed away from the door. The sound of his voice followed me down the hall like a low, persistent hum. By the time I reached the stairwell, my breath had gone shallow. I wasn't sure if it was because I'd been holding it or because I couldn't quite find it again. I told myself to breathe—in, two, three, four—out, two, three, four—but even that rhythm felt unsteady.

As I crossed the main hallway to head back to the parking lot, I passed the library. The sign taped to the glass door read OPEN ALL NIGHT FOR MIDTERMS.

Something tugged at me then. It was a small, certain knowing. Intuition, or maybe hope pretending to be intuition.

I pushed open the door. Inside, the lights were

low, the kind that hummed more than glowed. A handful of students huddled over laptops and textbooks, their faces bathed in the blue glow of screens.

And there, tucked into a corner near the math section, curled sideways in an armchair, a trigonometry textbook open across her knees, her red braid come half undone and the shadows under her eyes making her look older, though not old enough for what she was carrying—literally and otherwise—was Lila.

CHAPTER ELEVEN

The morning light in Stillwater was soft and syrupy as it pressed into my living room. I moved through the space quietly, barefoot, my breath matching the hush of the house. The guest room door was cracked open, just enough for me to peek inside.

Lila was asleep. She lay on her side, one arm tucked under her cheek, the other curved protectively over the swell of her belly. In the dim light, her freckles blurred into something tender and unfinished, like watercolor before it dries. Her breathing was slow and deep—the rhythm of someone who hadn't slept safely in a long time.

I stood in the doorway longer than I should've, just watching. The quilt had slipped down to her waist, revealing the small, round hill of her stomach beneath one of my old yoga shirts. It looked bigger this morning, or maybe I was just seeing it differently—seeing her differently.

That curve wasn't just a belly. It was possibility. A heartbeat I hadn't met yet but already felt tethered to.

A surprising ache unfurled in my chest. The feeling was warm, full, almost dizzying. I could already imagine the weight of that baby in my arms, the scent of powder and milk and innocence. I would give this child everything: patience, warmth, safety. All the softness this hard world forgets to offer.

Lila murmured something in her sleep and shifted, her fingers tightening over her belly. For just a second, she looked so young. Not the guarded, too-old teenager I'd met in that gray hallway but a girl—just a girl who should've been someone's child before she had to become someone's mother.

I wished her parents had loved her better.

Then, before I could stop myself, the darker thought surfaced—unwelcome and selfish.

If Lila's parents had loved her right... she wouldn't be here. She wouldn't be carrying this baby.

And I wouldn't be standing here, feeling this strange, fragile joy in the space between us.

I pressed a hand to my chest as if I could calm the guilt fluttering there. It was all so complicated. But I told myself it was for the best. Lila would have a chance to start over, to go to school, to become the woman she wanted to be. And I—

I would finally get to be the mother I'd always dreamed of being.

The house was quiet, just the faint hum of the refrigerator and the low chirp of morning birds outside. I turned toward the kitchen, thinking about tea, when a sudden knock shattered the stillness.

And then, before I could move—

"Tessa? You up?"

The door creaked open. I'd forgotten to lock it again. Darnell used to scold me for that—said Stillwater's charm made me careless. But this was my hometown. I knew everyone. What was there to fear?

I padded quickly down the hall, pressing a finger to my lips. "Lana, shh—"

Lana stood in the doorway, coffee in one hand, eyebrows raised in full mischief. She peered past me into the hallway like a cat looking for gossip.

"Why are we whispering?" she asked in a stage

whisper that was anything but quiet. "You've got company?"

My oldest friend's grin widened as my silence stretched a beat too long.

"Oh my God," she said, eyes gleaming. "You do. You've got a man in there, don't you?"

I blinked, momentarily stunned. "What? No, I—"

Lana gasped dramatically, pressing a hand to her heart. "Tessa Bloom! You little minx. Finally!"

My cheeks warmed. I could've told her the truth right then—that there was a scared, pregnant teen asleep in my guest room and that I was about to change my life in ways I hadn't dared to dream of in years. But I didn't.

And the question *why not?* rose up before I could push it down.

Maybe because I knew what Lana would say. She'd sip her coffee and tilt her head, the way she always did when she was about to deliver a hard truth. I'd hear the echo of the argument we'd had two decades ago— the one we still pretended never happened.

Lana had loved Darnell; everyone had. But she'd told me, gently at first and then not so gently, that I'd shrunk myself to fit his world. That I'd mistaken devotion for destiny. That everyone who knew me knew I'd wanted to be a mom one day. But I'd shoved that desire down for a man.

It was the only time we'd ever raised our voices to each other. Afterward, we'd both decided peace was more important than being right. We never mentioned it again.

So no, I didn't tell Lana about Lila. Or the baby. Or the ache that had come roaring back to life after all these years.

I smiled. Or maybe grimaced. "Yes, I have a guest over."

Lana squealed, the sound muffled behind her coffee cup. "About time, honey. I was beginning to think you'd die celibate."

I steered her gently toward the door, whispering a quick "We'll talk later."

"Oh, you will tell me everything. I want all the details. Dirty ones."

"Later," I said again.

When the door finally closed behind her, I leaned against it, pressing my forehead to the cool wood. The house was silent again. Peaceful. But beneath that quiet, my heart thrummed with something restless—hope, maybe, or fear dressed up as hope. Either way, I had the sudden feeling that peace, the kind I'd worked so hard to perfect, wasn't going to last much longer.

The door had barely clicked shut behind Lana when my phone started ringing. I jumped, heart leaping to my throat like a guilty teenager caught sneaking in after curfew. My eyes darted toward the hallway. Lila's door was still slightly ajar, the silence still intact. The last thing I needed was for the noise to wake her.

I snatched the phone off the counter and pressed it to my ear in a whisper. "Hello?"

"Tessa, it's Marianne."

Marianne's voice had that harried edge I'd come to recognize—like she was already halfway through an argument I hadn't heard the start of.

"I'm not going to be in the office this morning," she said without preamble. "I have to take over for my ex-husband, apparently."

I frowned, setting my mug down. "Is everything all right?"

"My son's pretending to be sick again," she huffed. "He does this sometimes. You know how kids are—they want attention. But of course, Hiro's too busy playing professor to go pick him up."

I pictured Hiro as I'd last seen him—steady, patient, with a baby tucked in one arm while he lectured with the other. Marianne was still going on, disparaging her ex-husband to me.

"…says he's busy. Meanwhile, I get the call from the school. Now I have to stop what I'm doing and interrupt my work."

I glanced at the clock. My morning was open; my first class wasn't until after lunch. I wanted that paperwork to go through. "If it would help, I could pick your son up for you and bring him to your office."

There was a pause on the line. "You'd do that?"

"Of course. I'm not far, and I know how these mornings can snowball."

Marianne exhaled, her irritation softening into weary gratitude. "That might actually work. Let me call the school and tell them you're coming."

"They all know me over there, anyway. I either grew up with the staff or taught half the mothers yoga at some point."

"You're a lifesaver, Tessa. I owe you."

"No debt. Just pay it forward with that paperwork."

"Deal. I'll have the forms ready by this afternoon. Come by anytime after four."

"You mean come by now to drop your son—"

But she had already hung up the phone.

CHAPTER TWELVE

The elementary school looked smaller than I remembered, the way everything from childhood does when you come back to it grown and grieving. The brick walls were still the same honeyed red, and the flag still flapped dutifully above the front steps, but the air smelled different—sweeter but cloyingly so. Probably from all the artificial dyes and additives they put in foods these days.

I parked beneath the old oak by the playground and sat for a moment, watching a group of kids tumble across the blacktop, laughing with that fearless abandon I used to envy even as a child. This place held ghosts. Not the kind that haunt. The kind that whispered to adults about times past.

Lana and I had met right there on that front

lawn, two third graders locked in a fierce debate over who got to be Princess Leia during recess. Celia had joined the next year, declaring herself our honorary Luke Skywalker because she refused to be "rescued." Bo Porter had come along with her and taken up the role of Han Solo, but he'd always looked at Celia like she was his Leia. Some loves take their time coming home.

And I'd had mine. Darnell Bloom had been the calm in my chaos, the steady to my scattered. I'd loved him loudly, deeply, with the sort of faith that didn't need fireworks to feel like forever. I was lucky for that, I knew.

Lana's teasing from that morning floated back to me. Her grin, her coffee cup raised in mock salute as she accused me of having a man tucked away in my house. Getting into another relationship had truly not occurred to me. I was happy on my own. Mostly.

Both Lana and Celia had found love again after heartbreak. I'd stood at each of their weddings, smiling so widely my cheeks ached, believing every word of the vows they'd spoken. They'd both been so sure back then. Hadn't they?

Both Lana and I had known Celia was settled—and settling for less than she deserved with a groom who looked at his phone with more longing than he looked at her. Lana had already begun to suspect her soon-to-be ex of cheating, but she'd gone ahead and married him so they could raise the baby in her belly. Then she went on to have two more buns in the oven before the timer went off in her marriage.

I'd been sure once, too. Darnell had been my certainty—steady, loyal, safe. I hadn't just loved him; I'd built my peace around him. When he died, it was like losing the gravity that kept me centered. And yet somehow I'd learned to stand again—balanced on my own breath.

Well, I had my girlfriends around me. It's easier to stand when you have two other legs, making you a human tripod.

Still, I wasn't made of stone. My body remembered what it felt like to be touched, to be seen. Sometimes, in the quiet hours, I missed the warmth of skin against mine, the weight of another heartbeat beside me.

But that was want, not love. Carnal, not sacred. I wasn't sure my heart could hold another man the way it had held Darnell. It felt too much like trying to plant something new in soil that had already been claimed by another's roots.

The thought of roots made me think of tall trees. The thought of tall trees made me think of Hiro

Tanaka. Those broad shoulders. Those impossibly dark eyes. The memory of his voice, low and steady while he'd rocked that baby in one arm like it was the most natural thing in the world.

Oh, my ovaries. They really needed to learn boundaries. Especially since they were well past their prime functioning years.

"Morning," said the receptionist, a round-faced woman with pink glasses.

"Morning, Jenny," I said with a grin. She'd sat behind me in choir for all four years of high school. "Still running the place, I see."

"Trying to," she laughed. "I got a message from Marianne Tanaka. You're here for her boy?"

I nodded.

Jenny gestured toward the row of chairs by the wall. Sam was there, small and slumped, shoulders hunched around a backpack almost bigger than him. His cheeks were pale, his dark eyes downcast. Whatever illness he'd claimed, it wasn't a fantasy.

"Sweet kid. Poor thing's sick more than he's well these days. Stress'll do that to a child. Especially when… well." Jenny tsked and shook her head, as though rearranging the thoughts she absolutely planned to share. "You know the Tanakas aren't from around here? Moved in last year. And divorced before Christmas."

"I—no, I didn't know that," I said carefully.

"There were parking lot arguments for months. That's how I knew it was bad. Walls got ears in this place, and the walls in a school? Positively chatty."

I remembered then why I'd kept my mouth shut during chorus unless it was to sing. Jenny was a songbird. She sang everyone else's tales to anyone who would listen.

"Half the teachers said they traded drop-offs like they were passing a hot potato. Sam crying some mornings, Ellie pitching fits others. That poor little thing spends more time in timeout than recess, from what I heard."

Jenny's tone suggested she'd heard it all from someone who'd heard it from someone who'd watched it with binoculars.

"Kids act out when the parents don't co-parent right. Funny thing, though—I didn't think the Tanakas had any family here. Not on her side, not on his. So I gotta ask..." Jenny's eyes sharpened with curiosity. "How do you know them?"

There it was. The sweet scent of gossip freshly blooming. I kept my posture open, my voice smooth, like I hadn't just stepped into a conversational minefield.

"I only met them recently," I said. "I'm just lending a neighborly hand today."

Jenny blinked, clearly waiting for more. When no more came, she made an interested hum under her breath—filed under Tessa Bloom: new gossip tangle —and slid a sign-in sheet toward me.

"Well, I hope everything settles down for those kids," she said. "Lord knows they deserve some stability."

I signed my name, the certainty settling into my bones. Yes. They deserved it. And maybe I could give them a little of it.

I walked over and crouched to Sam's level. "Hey, there," I said softly. "You must be Sam. I'm Tessa."

He blinked, studying me like a puzzle he half-remembered. "I know you from the cereal aisle."

"That's right," I said with a smile. "I'm a friend of your mom's. She couldn't make it, so she asked me to come get you. Is that okay?"

The little boy hesitated, fingers picking at the strap of his backpack. "Where are we going? Do I have to sit in her closet again?"

"Her... closet?" I echoed, thrown.

Sam nodded solemnly. "In her office at the end of

the hall. There's a computer in there that doesn't work and a desk, but nowhere to lie down."

Not a closet. A small office, probably—but still. The image of a little boy curled up between filing cabinets made my chest ache.

"How about you come rest at my place instead? It's quiet, and I've got a comfy couch that's really good for naps."

Sam thought about this, then nodded once, serious as a contract.

"Deal?" I said, holding out my hand.

He looked at it for a moment, then placed his small, warm fingers in mine. "Deal."

I rose, helping him to his feet. We'd barely taken two steps when a familiar voice—low, firm, and unmistakable—cut through the quiet.

"What exactly are you doing with my son?"

I turned, my breath catching before my heart had time to catch up.

Hiro Tanaka stood in the doorway, his tall frame filling it, his expression unreadable—those calm, dark eyes fixed squarely on me.

For a second, I forgot every soothing phrase I'd ever taught another human being. Because in that moment, I was the one who needed to breathe.

CHAPTER THIRTEEN

*H*iro Tanaka stood in the doorway, his tall frame outlined by the dull fluorescent light. His jaw was set, eyes sharp, shoulders squared like he was bracing for battle.

"What," he said quietly, "exactly are you doing with my son?"

The warmth that had been blooming in my chest vanished. I looked down at Sam, who'd instinctively loosened his grip on my hand, like I was the cookie he'd been trying to steal from the jar. I had to fight myself not to tighten my grip on him. This wasn't my kid. This wasn't even a play-nephew of mine. I wasn't his aunt. I was barely an acquaintance.

"Hi," I began carefully, forcing my voice into that soft, steady cadence I used with students who came to class angry at the world. "Sam's mom called me this morning."

Hiro's eyes tightened at attaching Sam to his mother. I wondered if his nostrils would've flared if I'd used Marianne's name. My mind went back to that closed-door argument back at Marianne's office. Her voice had been raised; his had not.

"Marianne said Sam wasn't feeling well—" And there went the nostril-flare. "And that she couldn't leave work. She asked if I could pick him up."

Hiro's jaw flexed, his eyes flicking to my brown hand joined with his son's paler one. His voice dropped even lower. He extended his hand toward his son. "Sam."

Sam hesitated, glancing at me—wide-eyed, uncertain. Then, slowly, he slipped his hand from mine and reached for his father's.

"Go wait in the hall," Hiro said gently, though the tension in his shoulders didn't ease. "The adults need to talk."

Sam looked between us, torn. "Dad, I—"

"It's okay," Hiro murmured, crouching for a second to meet his son's gaze. "You're not in trouble. I just need to speak with…"

Hiro looked expectantly at me.

"Tessa. Tessa Bloom."

"I just need to speak to Ms. Bloom. It doesn't concern children."

Sam nodded reluctantly and trudged toward the hall, his backpack bumping against his legs. When he disappeared around the corner, Hiro straightened, the kindness in his eyes evaporating as he turned back to me.

"How do you know Marianne?" His tone wasn't cruel—just clipped, precise, like he was interrogating a software glitch.

At the reception desk, Jenny wasn't even pretending not to watch. Her pink glasses glinted in the light as her gaze flicked between me and Hiro like she was watching the opening act of a particularly juicy drama. The soft, rhythmic tapping of her acrylic nails on the counter provided a soundtrack to our standoff. I bet she was just hitting the spacebar over and over again. Or typing out a transcript of our chat and posting it to the town's online forum.

Stillwater ran on gossip the way other towns ran on electricity—quietly, invisibly, but powering everything. By lunch, I had no doubt this little elementary school office tableau would be circulating from the post office to the pie shop.

Tessa Bloom caught arguing with Hiro Tanaka at the

elementary school. Passion ignited on the playground. The details would blur, the tone would sharpen, and by the end of the day, someone would swear they'd seen him dip me back and kiss me hard. That was small-town living for you. No secret stayed still for long.

I straightened my spine, smoothed the edges of my voice, and did what I'd been doing my whole life —performed serenity under pressure. "I know Marianne from…"

I was not about to admit that I was working with Marianne on my desire to adopt. Let the town think there was a torrid affair, a love triangle, a conspiracy plot even. But intent to become a mother was not fodder for the small town tabloids. That was not something I wanted the whole town to know anytime soon. Especially not when my best friends didn't even know.

"She's… a student of mine," I said finally. "At my studio. Springlight Yoga Retreat."

"Yoga?" Hiro repeated, as though testing the word for flaws.

I nodded, keeping my posture relaxed even though every nerve in my body wanted to shrink. "It's just down by Willow Creek. I was going to take Sam there and let him rest until she got off work. It's quiet, clean, peaceful. Better than a cramped office back at her job."

Hiro's eyes searched mine, dark and assessing. For a moment, I felt the full weight of his scrutiny. The man catalogued every breath, every word, as though he were running an internal diagnostic.

Then finally he sighed. "I appreciate your intention. But I'm here now. I'll take him back to my office."

Something in me resisted that. Maybe it was the memory of Sam's pallor, the way his head had drooped against the chair. Maybe it was instinct, or compassion, or the foolish belief that I could make things better.

I tilted my head slightly. "He doesn't look well. Maybe just a mild fever, but he's pale. If he's going to rest, wouldn't it be better to be somewhere quiet?"

Hiro's expression barely flickered, but I saw the faint twitch near his temple. It looked like the sign of a man too tired to argue but too proud to concede.

"There's construction at my house," he said finally. "Neither of us will get much peace there. Maybe I could work in the campus library..." He trailed off, gaze looking outside the window past Jenny, who had stopped typing and was openly texting on her bedazzled phone.

"You're both welcome at my studio. I don't have any yoga classes until late this afternoon. It's quiet there. Child-safe. Sam can nap while you work on my patio. It's serene and it has Wi-Fi."

"You're offering to watch my son? After meeting him once?"

I shrugged. "I'm great with kids. Around town, I'm everyone's auntie."

For some reason, I looked to Jenny for confirmation. Thank God she nodded enthusiastically, thumbs still tapping away as though she was relating every word to someone on the other end.

"It's what we do here in Stillwater. We take care of each other. You guys moved here a year ago?"

Hiro nodded. For a long moment, he said nothing. The silence stretched between us like a taut wire.

Then—so softly I almost missed it—he exhaled. "Fine. Thank you, Ms. Bloom."

"Tessa. My friends call me Tessa."

CHAPTER FOURTEEN

When I opened the door to the studio, the familiar scent of sandalwood and lemon balm rose to greet me. The scent was as soft and inviting as breath after a long hold. But this time, I tried to see the space through Hiro Tanaka's eyes.

What did he make of it? The wide expanse of honey-colored hardwood floors, the gauzy white curtains swaying in the slow rhythm of the ceiling fans, the gentle hum of the diffuser releasing lavender into the air. The room was meant to soothe, but I could feel the way he paused in the doorway. His stillness wasn't quite ease yet.

His son, though, was another story. Sam's eyes

went wide the moment he stepped inside. He took in the filtered light and the mural of water lilies painted across the far wall. His little shoulders, which had been tense and hunched on the walk from the car, softened instantly. The sight made me smile before I could stop myself.

"I like it," he said.

"Thanks." I grinned, then glanced up at his father.

Hiro stood a few feet behind him, his posture precise as a line of code. His hands were in his pockets, chin slightly lifted, scanning the space like a man cataloging potential hazards. But I saw it, the almost imperceptible loosening of his jaw, the way his chest expanded on a long, deliberate inhale. Ease... incoming.

I led them toward the back of the retreat center, where the windows opened to a wide view of Stillwater Lake, its surface rippling with morning light. The back room was my favorite place in the world. Plush couches, woven throws, shelves lined with plants that always seemed to lean toward the glass as if hungry for reflection.

Sam gave a delighted little gasp and hurried ahead, pressing his hands against the window. "It looks like the water's glowing!"

I smiled, unable to help it. "It does that some-times. Depends on the clouds and the angle of the sun."

Behind him, Hiro inhaled again—deeper this time. His shoulders dropped half an inch. The sound, small as it was, felt like victory. It was getting easier.

"Make yourselves comfortable," I said, gesturing toward the couches. "I'll make you both some tea."

"That's not necessary," Hiro said quickly, voice smooth and measured. It was like the ease had sucked itself back into his chest.

"It's no trouble," I assured him, moving toward the kitchenette. "I've got a medicinal blend that should help Sam's stomach. And I'll put a honey stick in his cup."

Sam turned to look at his father, his expression cautious, like he'd learned to wait for permission before wanting anything.

Hiro's gaze softened just enough to make some-thing tighten in my chest. He gave a single nod. That was all it took for Sam's face to light up.

I left the room and filled the kettle. Then turned and reached for the jars of herbs lined neatly along the counter. Chamomile for calm. Peppermint for ease. Ginger for warmth. The ingredients were simple, but the ritual of blending them—of caring through small, intentional acts—always steadied me.

As the kettle began to hum, I caught a glimpse of their reflections in the glass. Sam, small and eager, his feet barely touching the floor as he sank into the couch. Hiro beside him, composed but watching his son with that quiet kind of vigilance that said everything he didn't.

Sam sniffled. His father lifted a hand and pressed the back of his fingers to the boy's forehead—gentle, practiced, sure. The kind of touch that came from years of knowing his child's body better than any thermometer. Sam leaned into it instinctively, like this was their language.

After settling Sam, Hiro opened a brown leather briefcase and took out a stack of paperwork, the motion efficient but unhurried. Then he slid a pencil behind his ear. It was such a small, ordinary gesture, but it gave me a little thrill. I'd had a weakness for that quiet kind of authority ever since I was a girl.

In fifth grade, I was hopelessly smitten with Mr. Carver, my gym teacher—tall, tanned, and endlessly patient with a line of gangly girls pretending to stretch while sneaking glances at his whistle. He'd tell us to breathe through the burn, and even then I thought, what a lovely way to live.

In high school, it was Mr. Sandoval, my art teacher. He wore paint-splattered shirts and spoke about color like it was a language only the brave could understand. Once he'd leaned over my shoulder to correct the curve of a brushstroke, and I'd forgotten how to breathe properly for a full minute.

Then in college—Professor Harding. History. He quoted Rilke and looked at his students as though every one of us was capable of brilliance. I'd written an extra paper that semester just to have a reason to linger after class.

And now here I was, decades later, still reacting to the sight of a man with a pencil behind his ear.

The kettle began to sing—a soft, rising hum that filled the quiet space with the sound of something about to overflow. I moved slowly, methodically, trying to center myself in the ritual. Chamomile. Peppermint. Ginger. A touch of honey. Small acts of care, simple and steady, the way peace was supposed to be.

My phone buzzed on the counter.

Celia.

"Hey, you ready for our lunch date?" Her voice

was bright, warm, and entirely unprepared for my lapse.

Lunch date? Right. The little Italian place near the square.

"Oh—Celia," I said, forcing cheer into my tone. "I'm so sorry, I—uh—I can't today. I've got some work to do at the studio, and I completely lost track of time."

There was a pause. Then, "That's fine. I'll just bring over takeout."

"No, no, don't. I'm just… buried under things right now. I'm not going to get out from under it anytime soon."

"Oh."

It was a small sound, but it carried decades of uncertainty. I'd heard that particular *oh* from her many times before. Ever since we were teenagers, and she'd caught me and Lana whispering about something silly, something she wasn't part of. It wasn't jealousy so much as fear. Fear of being left out. Of not belonging.

I closed my eyes, pressing a hand to my chest. "Hey, Celia. It's not that I don't want to see you, I promise. Can we do tomorrow? Or maybe the weekend? I just—today's not good timing."

There was a shuffling on her end, the sound of

her sigh. "Sure," she said softly. "Whenever is good for you."

Before I could say more, a low voice came from behind me.

"I'll take that cup of tea after all."

Hiro stood a few feet away, one hand in his pocket, the other resting on the counter. There was a half-smile on his face. In the face of it, it felt like sunlight finding its way through a crack.

"Oh," I said stupidly, the word escaping before I could tame it.

He nodded once, the faintest dip of acknowledgment, and turned to walk back toward the lounge where Sam sat curled up under an afghan.

My heart beat a little too loudly in the quiet that followed.

On the phone, Celia let out a delighted squeal. "Oh my God. Lana was right! You do have a man over there, don't you?"

I blinked, my gaze lingering on Hiro's broad shoulders as he settled back on the couch, taking the pencil from behind his ear. I could have told Celia the truth—that it was nothing like that, that there was a sick child and a favor and an uncomfortable sort of tension with the single dad that I hadn't figured out how to name.

But truth required energy, and I was already stretched thin trying to balance serenity and chaos in the same breath.

So instead, I smiled into the receiver and said lightly, "You caught me."

CHAPTER FIFTEEN

I actually did have work to do in the studio. I needed to finalize the weekend retreat schedule, update the billing software, and replant the wilting pothos by the front desk. There was a shipment of yoga bolsters to unpack, too, and the endless, meditative folding of clean blankets that always made me feel both productive and serene.

But every few minutes, my eyes drifted toward Hiro Tanaka.

He'd taken over one of the low tables near the window on the open screened patio where I some-times held meditation classes. He didn't sit with a manspread. Those long legs did take up space, though. His laptop rested on his thighs, glasses perched on the bridge of his nose. Sam sat nearby, pale but content beneath a knitted throw.

I brought over a small tray—orange slices, buttered croissants from the office fridge, and two mugs of tea. I'd told myself the tray was for Sam, but the boy was drowsy, and I'd sliced enough oranges for two.

"Here we go." I set the tray on the table. "Vitamin C, a little comfort, and something warm."

Sam smiled faintly, eyes half-closed. I tucked the blanket around him, smoothing it over his small frame, brushing a stray lock of hair from his forehead. When I looked up, Hiro was watching me, like he was studying code and trying to understand the pattern.

"You have a real maternal instinct," he said quietly.

I gave a small laugh, one that sounded steadier than I felt. "My mother warned me about that. She said I came from a long line of women with soft hearts and open arms. She used to joke that I'd end up with a house full of children."

Hiro nodded once, his gaze flicking briefly to his son, then back to me. "How many do you have?"

The question was simple. The answer was not.

"None." The word lingered in the air between us —small but sharp, a truth that never lost its edge.

He didn't say anything, didn't rush to fill the silence. His quiet was patient. And maybe that's why I kept talking.

"I'm going to adopt."

His brows lifted slightly, but his expression didn't change. He didn't say *you're too old* or *why now*. He just waited—steady, open, listening.

I exhaled slowly, looking down at the little boy sleeping on my studio couch. "I spent years fighting it, that prediction of my mother's. I thought I was different—that I could love deeply without needing to mother anyone. But... I've always been that person. The one who takes care of everyone else's kids. My friends', my students'. And now that I can't make one of my own, that's all I want. Isn't that ridiculous?"

Hiro shook his head. "Not ridiculous. It's very logical. It just takes some people longer to recognize who they are. What they truly want. Sometimes we fight our own programming because of a bug in the system."

I arched a brow. "Are you calling me a bug?"

"No." He chuckled, low and quiet, the sound vibrating through the calm like a warm note. "I'm saying something—or someone—introduced the wrong line of code. It takes time to debug. But once you do, the system runs true again."

I looked down, tracing the rim of my mug with a finger. The wrong line of code. Hiro wasn't wrong. My love for Darnell had been the bug—a beautiful one, a necessary one, but one that had rewritten parts of me I'd only just begun to reclaim.

I glanced up again. Hiro was watching me still, the faintest smile lingering in his eyes, and for the first time, I didn't look away.

Hiro sat back, the light from the window catching the edges of his glasses as he studied his son. Sam's breathing had evened out, soft and rhythmic beneath the weight of the blanket.

"I didn't want kids," Hiro said quietly.

The words surprised me—not because they were harsh but because they were spoken with such tenderness. His gaze stayed on his son, his voice low and even, like he was narrating a story he'd already made peace with.

"Marianne did," he went on. "And I was in love with her, so… I gave her what she wanted."

Hiro smiled faintly then, the kind of smile that didn't reach his eyes but somehow reached his heart. "And then I fell hard for him. For both of them. Sam first, then Ellie. They completely rewrote my code. A complete new program that I was unprepared for, and no amount of reading all the data and research and anecdotes could prepare me for. But they made me a better man. Or a better machine."

He said it like an admission, but it sounded more like reverence.

I blinked, unsure what to say. His phrasing—the code, the rewrite—it was so measured. Logical. And yet everything about the way he looked at that sleeping boy was pure emotion.

Hiro sighed, pinching the bridge of his nose as though bracing himself for impact. "Marianne will probably be here soon."

He said it like a soldier noting enemy movement. Calm. Inevitable.

I wondered what had gone wrong between them. They had built a family together, shared love once. Yet even in the quiet peace of my studio, tension followed his every breath like a shadow.

Hiro stood, shoulders straightening beneath his pressed shirt. "I'd better get going and get Sam to her. Ellie has a sleepover tonight. The contractors are almost done at my house."

I looked at Sam, small and serene under the blanket. Then I looked at Hiro—the stress returning to his face, the tightness settling back into his posture.

"You know," I said softly, "Marianne was planning to come by here to get Sam, anyway. We could just stick with that plan. She doesn't know you're here. You could... go. Let her pick him up from me."

Hiro paused, hand hovering near his briefcase.

"You can see I'm not going to kidnap your son," I added, smiling faintly. "Especially not with all those germs he's probably spreading around."

Hiro turned then, one eyebrow raised. "Are you saying my kid isn't worthy of kidnapping?"

It was a tease—a dry, quiet kind of humor—but when he smiled, it was devastating. A real smile this time. It cracked through my practiced calm like sunlight through stained glass. It tickled at the edge of my heart. No, that was my boob. The nipple on my left boob went instantly erect.

Now, I could chalk that up to perimenopause. Since turning forty-five, my periods had become irregular, and my boobs had started itching. Underneath, on the sides, around the areolas. These were symptoms of The Change, my OBGYN had told me. Just something else I had no say in but had to get used to.

Only my boobs weren't itching. Was that an ache? Was that… interest?

I hadn't realized how long it had been since I'd been attracted to anyone. The thought startled me. I'd loved Darnell with every part of me, and when he died, I'd quietly decided that part of my life was over. But standing here, watching Hiro—stern, steady, unexpectedly gentle—I felt that long-dormant spark flicker awake. In my boobs.

"You can trust me," I said softly, trying to steady my tone and ignore my breasts.

He looked at me then—really looked.

For a moment, I thought I was flashing head-lights. I couldn't look down to check.

After a long moment, he nodded. "I do."

Hiro reached up, took the pencil from behind his ear, and placed it carefully in his briefcase before closing it with a quiet click. Then he turned toward the door.

I followed him, my steps matching his until we reached the front of the studio together.

He turned abruptly, and suddenly we were face to face. Close enough that I could smell the faint hint of cedar and clean linen clinging to him. We were close enough to share the same air. Close enough that I could see the faint stubble along his jaw, smell the clean, crisp scent of his soap. My heart gave a single, traitorous thud.

Then he stepped back. "You're a good friend," he said, his voice quieter now. Then, after a beat, "To Marianne. She needs good friends."

I nodded, forcing a small, agreeable smile.

Of course, she did. And that's what I was—a friend. To her. Not to him.

The truth was, people always took sides when a marriage cracked open. And whether I liked it or not, my seed had been sown on her side.

CHAPTER SIXTEEN

By the time the sun began to dip low over Stillwater Springs, my body hummed with the familiar ache of motion, but my mind was elsewhere. It was half on the boy asleep in the next room and half on the clock that kept marking time without a knock at my door.

Marianne was late.

Not just a few minutes late—the kind of late that pressed against politeness and started whispering worry into my ear. I'd finished my last Savasana fifteen minutes ago. My students had gone, their soft laughter trailing down the hall. I'd tidied the mats, folded the blankets, watered the plants. Still no call. No text.

Sam had woken up an hour earlier, still a little

pale but smiling when I offered him a snack. He'd eaten two orange slices and a croissant, then politely asked if he could "rest a little more." How could I say no to those kind of manners?

By late afternoon, I decided to take him home.

Normally, I walked the few blocks between my studio and the little cottage I lived in. The path wound past the bakery, then the row of maples that always smelled faintly of sap. But Sam's steps had grown smaller by the minute, his hand warm and damp in mine, so I opted for the car instead. Even short distances can feel like mountains when a fever is around.

The drive took less than two minutes, past familiar storefronts and onto my quiet street. My cottage sat at the end, white siding and blue shutters, small enough to look hugged by its own porch. I'd shared that house with Darnell. I still remembered the day we bought it—how I'd insisted on being close enough to the lake to hear it hum. Stillwater had always been my favorite place in the world, and the lake's soft babbling was my favorite sound aside from my husband's laughter.

After he passed, the lake became my anchor. On nights when the grief pressed too hard against my ribs, I'd open the windows and let the water speak to me. I never once dreamed of selling the cottage. Instead, I used the money Darnell left to buy the larger property down the road—the one that became my yoga retreat. The cottage was my heart; the retreat was the dream I built to survive its breaking.

I pulled onto the gravel drive and helped Sam out of the car. His small fingers curled around mine with surprising trust.

Inside, the house held its usual warmth—soft lamplight, lavender lingering in the air, the faint whisper of the lake through the cracked kitchen window.

Lila was curled up on the couch with a math workbook when we walked in. Her eyes widened when she saw Sam. She didn't ask questions. Just smiled in that shy, uncertain way of hers and moved her books aside so he could sit.

"I'll be right back," I told her. "Keep an eye on him for me?"

I went back to the studio to teach my final class, but it was hard to stay centered. My words came out automatically—"Breathe in, release, let go"—but my mind kept circling back to my house. To the way Hiro had smiled at me when I handed him the honey stick. Then to the empty quiet of my phone.

I'd texted Marianne that her son was at my

house, along with the address. She still hadn't reached out.

I considered calling Hiro, but I didn't have his number. Even if I did, what would I say? *Your son's fine, your ex-wife's missing in action, and I've got both of them covered?*

It wasn't a hardship. Sam was a delight. Quiet. Thoughtful. By the time I returned home after my class, he and Lila were bent over a jigsaw puzzle with the faint hum of cartoons playing in the background. After a dinner of jerk chicken over rice and beans, seasoned greens, and plantains, the boy, who'd looked half-sick this morning, now looked entirely well-fed, well-rested, and—if I was honest— well-loved. Lila's cheeks looked pinker, her belly fuller—if that was possible.

I'd just started to wash the dishes when headlights swept across the living room curtains. Then came the sound of a car door closing, followed by brisk footsteps up the walk. A moment later, a knock rapped at the front door.

Lila looked up from the couch. Sam, too. I dried my hands, smoothed my hair, and tried to arrange my features into something between calm and welcoming, though a flicker of annoyance threaded through the serenity I practiced like scripture.

Marianne's knock came again, sharp and impatient. But hadn't she been the one making me, her son, and her ex-husband wait? When I opened the door, she was all smiles—wide, bright, and just a shade too shiny to be real. Her hair was windblown, her blouse rumpled, and the faint scent of alcohol rode beneath her perfume, sharp and citrusy.

"Tessa!" she said, exhaling my name like relief. "I am so sorry I'm late. Things at work just… spiraled."

"Come in," I said, smoothing my voice into calm neutrality.

She stepped past me, the click of her heels loud against my hardwood floors. Her eyes darted around the room, landing first on Sam, who'd been sitting cross-legged beside Lila on the couch, working on the same puzzle they'd been piecing together for the past hour.

"Hi, Mom," Sam said, subdued. He didn't move toward her right away.

Marianne swooped down, arms flung wide. "There's my little man!" she gushed, pressing loud kisses to his hair and cheeks. "Oh, honey, I missed you so much. Did you miss me? Tell me you missed me."

Sam's face pinched. His small shoulders tensed

beneath her touch. He nodded his head like an obedient pet.

Marianne cupped his face and kissed him again. "Silly boy."

There was affection there, yes—but it came out too forcefully, like someone trying to make up for absence with volume. And then her gaze caught on Lila.

For a heartbeat, Marianne's expression faltered. "Oh," she said, blinking. "You're here? Before the paperwork is finalized." Her gaze swung back to me, entirely sober.

Lila rose quickly, tugging at her oversized hoodie. "I can grab my stuff and go. Sorry if—"

"No, no," Marianne interrupted, her smile snapping back into place. "It's just… technically, it's not appropriate for you to be here before the paperwork's finalized. We could get into trouble for that, you know."

Lila froze, eyes wide.

"Right now, Lila's a friend staying over at my place." I turned to Lila. "And if it truly becomes a problem, I'll pay for a hotel."

"No need for any of that. We're all friends here." Marianne's gaze flicked to me, the corners of her mouth tightening a second before she smoothed it over with another too-sweet smile. She turned back to Lila, tone softening. "Don't worry about it, sweetheart. I won't say a word. In fact, I'll make sure to push the paperwork through as fast as I can."

Marianne's hand found Lila's arm in a quick pat that was meant to reassure but only made the girl flinch.

"Thank you," Lila murmured.

Marianne nodded, already moving on, already back to performance. She turned to me with that dazzling, brittle smile that didn't quite reach her eyes. "Actually, Tessa—since you've been so wonderful with Sam, I was wondering if you might do me one more favor?"

My stomach tightened.

"Are you free this Friday night? I've got to stay late at work, and you know how it is—no rest for the weary. It'd really help me out if you took both Sam and his sister. It'll give me time to get that paperwork moving."

Her words hung there, light and casual but weighted beneath the surface.

I looked past her—to Sam, now fidgeting with his shoelaces, to Lila, who'd sunk quietly back onto the couch, pretending to study the puzzle again.

I smiled, the same calm, steady smile I'd given

hundreds of times before when a student confessed an affair after deep pranayama breathing, or a friend broke down after finding out their significant other was cheating, or when a stranger mistook my peace for permission to get something over on me.

"Of course," I said finally. "If it helps move the paperwork along."

Marianne's grin brightened, almost wolfish. "Perfect. I knew I could count on you."

As she herded her son toward the door, I caught one last whiff of perfume and wine and exhaustion. When the door closed behind them, the silence that followed was thick enough to touch.

Lila looked up at me, eyes questioning.

I exhaled slowly, steadying my breath. "It's fine," I said. "Everything's fine."

But it wasn't peace I felt. It was the faint, familiar tremor of a storm I was pretending not to see.

CHAPTER SEVENTEEN

Bo's house smelled like cedar and something savory—probably whatever he'd grilled for lunch before the meeting. The fire crackled in the stone hearth, and a light rain drifted lazily outside the big bay window. It was the kind of cozy domestic scene Hallmark movies built entire empires on.

Belle sat at the head of the table, running the meeting with her usual polished efficiency, her tablet propped against a mug of peppermint tea. Zach hung on her every word like she was reading from a sacred text. Bo, meanwhile, couldn't stop gazing at Celia, who pretended not to notice but was absolutely aware of it.

By the time Belle closed her notes and announced the final agenda item—vendor confirmations for the Summer Bazaar—the men were checking their phones for score updates on whatever sports ball was at halftime or quarters or whatever, and Lana was doodling holly leaves in the margins of her notepad. Zach immediately volunteered to help Belle clean up. Bo's phone rang, and he ducked into the other room to answer it.

Lana nudged me as we watched them go. "You know, this place finally feels like Celia lives here."

Celia laughed softly. "Well, considering half my throw blankets and every scented candle I own have migrated here, I'd say that's fair."

I glanced around. She wasn't wrong. Bo's house—once all dark wood and bachelor austerity—had softened. There were cozy touches everywhere: a knit blanket draped over the couch, framed photos of their grown kids, a vase of winter roses by the window. It looked like a home. But as my eyes traced the room, I couldn't help but see the faint ghosts of how it used to look.

I'd been here before—years ago, when Billie Porter was still alive. Darnell and I had come for holiday parties, back when laughter and the scent of mulled wine filled these rooms. I could still picture her—Billie—gliding through the space with her gold bracelets chiming, her red lipstick perfect, her presence as curated as her décor.

Billie had impeccable taste—cool tones, sharp edges, everything polished to a magazine shine. The kind of house where the throw pillows never left their assigned corners and not a single object existed without purpose or symmetry. And Bo…

Bo had always looked the slightest bit out of place in it. Not unhappy—never that—but like a man standing inside the life someone else had arranged for him. A little too big for the delicate furniture. A little too warm for all that glass and steel. Hands in his pockets, smile polite, posture careful—as if one wrong move might disturb the tableau.

Everything had been picture perfect. Picture perfect marriage. Picture perfect holidays. Picture perfect silence where any messiness might have been.

Now?

Now the house was lived in. The air felt softer, the colors warmer, the edges rounded by use. Blankets draped themselves over couch arms. A pair of sneakers leaned against the baseboard. Someone, probably Celia, had left a stack of books on the coffee table. The whole place breathed in a way it never had before.

And the two people who spent the most time inside it… they looked relaxed, and settled, and tired, and happy. So very happy. The kind of happiness that isn't staged or styled or performed but grown—uneven and real—out of late nights, early mornings, shared burdens, small victories, and the quiet grace of simply choosing each other.

For the first time, Bo didn't look like a man in someone else's picture. He looked like he belonged. Because he and Celia belonged together.

Celia looked lighter, too. The tough corners that had always bracketed her gaze were rounded out. The color palette of her clothes had warmed. Celia's light was bright enough to chase away shadows, even the long ones left behind by memory.

And yet, for one small, aching moment, I felt a pang of sorrow for Billie. It wasn't jealousy—not exactly. It was… empathy. The quiet kind that comes from realizing someone's presence was being overwritten by someone else's happiness.

I wondered if that was what it would be like for me, too. If someday, some man might walk into the little house Darnell and I had built together—might repaint the walls, rearrange the furniture, fill the rooms with new laughter.

The thought made my chest tighten.

I'd told myself for years that I'd made peace with being alone. That the kindest thing I could do for Darnell's memory was keep it undisturbed, a shrine no one else could touch. But as I looked at the glow of Celia's candles flickering against Bo's dark wood, I couldn't decide if she'd desecrated something sacred… or if she'd saved it from fading away.

Maybe both.

"So what's the plan?" Lana asked. "Are you and Bo going to sell one of your houses now that you're basically living together?"

Celia shook her head. "No, neither of us wants to. The mortgages are paid off, and we both have too many memories tied up in both places. Zach's still living with me anyway. It works. I spend most of my time here, but I like knowing the old house is there."

I smiled at that—sentimentality disguised as practicality. Typical Celia.

"All done with cleanup," Belle said as she and Zach came back into the living room. "I've got to run —I've got a date."

The room stilled for a heartbeat. Celia, Lana, and

I turned toward Zach with matching hopeful smiles. Zach's expression crumpled like paper.

"Oh," he said softly. "Nice. Cool. Have fun."

Belle flashed him a friendly grin, oblivious. "See you tomorrow."

When the door closed behind her, the silence that followed was thick enough to chew.

Bo reappeared, slipping his phone into his pocket. "Zach, I'm meeting Theo at the bar. You want to join us?"

Zach sighed, rubbing a hand over his jaw. "Sure. Why not?"

And just like that, the men were gone, leaving the three of us alone in the quiet warmth of Bo's living room.

Lana looked around at the half-empty wine glasses and sighed. "You know, the wine selection here isn't great. Let's go to Tessa's. She always has the good stuff."

"We can't."

Both of them turned toward me in unison. "Why not?"

Lana's grin spread slow and knowing. "Oh my God. You're having someone over, aren't you?"

Celia gasped. "Tessa!"

I tried to look affronted, but my cheeks betrayed

me with heat. "No, I—"

They started to laugh, talking over me, their teasing overlapping in a familiar rhythm.

"Look at her, she's glowing," Lana said. "It's about time."

"I'm not glowing," I protested. "And I'm not—well—I'm not ready to talk about it."

Celia held up her hands. "Fine. We'll stop prying. For now."

"Just don't think that gets you out of girls' night on Friday," Lana added. "We already have reservations. You can't bail."

I winced, my stomach sinking. I'd completely forgotten.

"I can't," I said, trying for apologetic but landing somewhere closer to guilty. "I have… a date."

Lana groaned. "Oh, come on. We never ditched you when we started dating."

"I know, I know." I exhaled, pinching the bridge of my nose. "Just give me this one time. It won't happen again."

They exchanged a look that was equal parts skepticism and affection.

"Fine," Lana said finally. "But we expect details afterward."

"Every last one," Celia added.

I smiled, hoping they couldn't hear the quiet thud of my heart—or the tiny voice in the back of my mind whispering that what awaited me on Friday night wasn't a date at all but a favor I wasn't sure I should have agreed to.

CHAPTER EIGHTEEN

I'd thought a walk by the water might help calm the Tanaka kids. You know—fresh air, open space, the steady hush of Stillwater Lake breathing against its banks. The cool, clean sand was tinged with the mineral tang of freshwater and the faint sweetness of decaying leaves. The light shimmered across the surface in long, trembling ribbons, as if the lake were trying to soothe anyone who walked beside it.

It soothed me after a Friday morning of Mommy and Me yoga, a 90-minute Hot Yoga session, and a challenging Yin Yoga session.

It soothed Sam, too. His shoulders dropped the moment we stepped onto the narrow trail. He bent to touch the sand with his fingertips, letting the grains sift through like tiny beads. When the breeze carried the scent of damp earth and sun-warmed pine toward us, he inhaled like it was medicine.

The soothing stopped and turned the other way went it came up against Ellie Tanaka.

Even after a full day of school, she was still a ball of kinetic energy—pure motion wrapped in a pink jacket. She darted ahead on the path, her laugh ringing across the water like a skipping stone. Pebbles flew from her hands, splashing into the lake with tiny plunks that startled the minnows along the shoreline. Then she was climbing, wobbling, windmilling her arms atop a half-submerged rock, daring gravity to come and get her.

"Ellie," I called gently. "Feet on the ground, please."

She giggled, all curls and defiance. "I'm a fairy, Ms. Tessa. Fairies don't walk."

Behind me, Sam groaned under his breath. "You're gonna fall in," he muttered. His shoulders were already curling inward, his jaw set in that way kids have when they've carried too much responsibility for too long.

I slowed my pace until I was beside him. "You okay?"

He shrugged, eyes fixed on his sister. "She never listens."

"She's got a lot of energy. Let's give her some more time to wiggle it out of her system before we go inside."

He didn't answer. His hands flexed at his sides, like he was torn between worry and weariness. Every time Ellie splashed too close to the edge, he flinched, as if he were the one about to fall.

"Ellie," he said, sharper this time. "Dad said no climbing near the water!"

"I'm not climbing," she sang back. "I'm pretending."

A gull cried overhead, punctuating the tension.

I took a deep breath and tried for calm authority —the kind that worked to get a new student into an unassisted inverted posture like a headstand. "Ellie, sweetheart, how about we pretend to be fairies on land for a while? I think the water sprites are feeling a little crowded."

That earned me a squint. "Water sprites?"

I nodded solemnly. "They get grumpy when humans invade their space. Especially the noisy ones."

For a moment, she actually considered this. Then

she stomped back toward us, pouting but intrigued. "Can I be their queen instead?"

"Queen? Not a princess?"

"My mommy says big girls are queens. Princesses are babies. I'm a big girl."

"Of course," I said. "Queen Ellie of the Sprites."

"Ms. Tessa, I don't think you should let her do that."

I smiled down at Sam. "You don't have to be her keeper, Sam. Just her brother."

He frowned at that, uncertainty flickering in his eyes.

"You can splash a little too if you like. I trust you. You're very good with the rules."

The wind shifted, cool and gentle off the lake. I reached out and brushed a hand through his hair. It was something maternal and instinctive, something I didn't stop myself from doing. "I've got her," I said. "You go play for a bit."

Sam hesitated, then nodded slowly. He went to the water's edge and toed it, but he didn't splash.

We walked on like that for a while; Ellie skipping ahead again but on the path this time, narrating her fairy kingdom in bursts of imagination. Sam trudged quietly beside me, the tension in his small body easing little by little.

For dinner, I made spaghetti with a simple sauce, the kind my mother used to throw together on nights when she didn't have much energy but still wanted to feed love into the room.

Sam sat at the table, posture careful, polite as always. He twirled a forkful of noodles, quiet and observant, like he was waiting to take emotional cues before he dared breathe too loud. Ellie, meanwhile, had her chin in her hand and a pout that could curdle milk.

"I don't want it," she said. "It's not how Daddy makes it."

"Well, I'm not your father, but I tried my best."

She didn't look impressed. Her fork scraped at the noodles without touching them. Her legs swung beneath the chair, building up tension like a wind-up toy about to break loose.

"I don't like it."

"You haven't even tasted it. Will you give it a try?"

"I said I don't like it!"

Her small hand flipped the plate. It spun once—almost gracefully, like a fluttering fairy flitting about—before clattering across the table and skidding onto the floor, splattering sauce in bright red streaks across my clean tile.

The silence that followed was thick. Heavy. It

reminded me of spaghetti noodles going soft in boiling water—plumping from brittle, breakable sticks into something limp and swollen, dense enough to tangle, impossible to ignore. A silence you had to wade through. A silence that made everything else—the ticking of the clock, the hum of the refrigerator—sound too loud.

It stretched between us, elastic and fragile, waiting for the first person to breathe wrong and snap it.

Sam groaned, already sliding off his chair to grab a rag from the counter. The kid moved with the kind of weary efficiency that told me this wasn't new.

Ellie sat there, arms crossed, a triumphant little smirk tugging at her mouth—as if to say *your move, Ms. Tessa.*

I drew in a slow breath through my nose. In yoga, we call it ujjayi breathing—breath that sounds like the sea, meant to cool the body and clear the mind. It did neither.

"I'm disappointed in your behavior, Ellie. That wasn't kind, and it certainly wasn't respectful—" I didn't even make it to the part about consequences before she crumbled.

Her face folded, her lower lip trembled, and

suddenly she was hiccupping through sobs. "You're mad at me! You don't love me anymore!"

"Ellie—sweetheart, no, that's not—"

But she was gone, spiraling into tears so big they swallowed every ounce of composure I had. Sam just kept cleaning, not looking at either of us. The rag made soft circles on the floor while his sister's cries filled the room.

I stood there, frozen between wanting to comfort her and wanting to walk out onto the porch to breathe.

Lana's girls had thrown fits, of course, but never like this. Their rebellions were mild—an eye roll, a slammed door, a half-hearted pout that melted with a snack. Zach had his anxiety, but even as a kid, he'd always tried so hard to please. Belle at that age would have been the one ordering others to wipe up the mess and giving the lecture on proper manners.

My nieces and nephews wouldn't have dreamed of throwing food—not in their parents' houses, and definitely not in their grandmother's. But they were all grown.

Was this just kids these days? Or was this what happened when their parents got divorced and their world fell apart?

But no, Lana had gotten divorced, and her kids were… fine. At least in my opinion, if not hers.

I looked at Sam—still quietly scrubbing at the sauce, trying to erase his sister's outburst before it left a mark—and my throat tightened. I stared at Ellie, red-faced and sobbing, and for the first time since I'd filled out the adoption paperwork, doubt flickered in my chest.

Would Lila's baby throw tantrums like this one day?

Would I know what to do when she did?

CHAPTER NINETEEN

I woke to the soft blue glow of the television and the brittle ache in my neck that comes from falling asleep somewhere a woman my age shouldn't. The cartoon on the screen had long since lost its plot. What remained was a looping world of color and noise meant to soothe small, restless minds.

Sam was a curled comma of sleep on the floor, one arm flung protectively toward his sister. Ellie, on the other hand, was still wide awake. Her eyes were glassy and fixed on the screen. Her little body was wound tightly in the cocoon of blankets they'd built earlier. At least she was quiet.

The faint ping of my phone cut through the hush. I reached for it, blinking at the screen's light. 12:07

a.m. The message preview read: *Marianne Tanaka.* My stomach tightened before I even opened it, sensing what I already knew hours ago.

Hey, Tessa. Grabbed a few drinks with coworkers. Not up for driving. I'll swing by early in the morning to get the kids. Also finished that paperwork.

I exhaled slowly through my nose, trying to release the irritation before it could harden into something uglier.

A few drinks. Not up for driving. Finished the paperwork.

The words blurred together like she was doing me a favor instead of leaving me stranded with two children who weren't mine—one who never stopped moving and one who never stopped worrying.

I set the phone face down on my chest, staring at the ceiling. The wood beams above me looked steady and sure, the opposite of how I felt.

Why couldn't she have just asked? A simple, "Tessa, would you mind keeping them overnight?" would've been fine. I closed my eyes and tried to remind myself—breathe in, breathe out, no one benefits from resentment. But the air caught somewhere behind my ribs.

Lila had come home earlier from her night class, buzzing about equations and theorems I couldn't begin to understand. I'd made her tea and sent her to bed, promising to keep the house quiet. There was no way I could ask her to help with Ellie in the morning. Not when she was carrying so much—literally and otherwise.

By the time dawn broke, the cartoon was still murmuring in the background, and my brain felt like it had been stretched too thin between responsibility and exhaustion.

Seven a.m. came and went. No Marianne. No text. No call.

I stared at my phone, willing it to buzz. Nothing.

I wasn't angry, not exactly. Just… tired of cleaning up other people's chaos under the guise of compassion.

Still, something had to be done. I couldn't keep the kids through the day. I had a sunrise class in less than an hour. So I did what I should've done last night. I called Belle.

"Hey," she answered, already sounding awake and efficient.

"Sorry to bother you this early, sweetheart," I said, trying to sound calm and not like a woman on the verge of losing her serenity. "Do you happen to have Hiro Tanaka's number? I know you sold him a house last year."

There was a pause on the line. "Everything okay?"

"I bumped into him and his son yesterday, and his son left something at my yoga studio." It wasn't a lie. Not exactly. I had bumped into Hiro and Sam. They had been at my yoga studio. And now something was left behind. All true. Just woven together haphazardly and out of context.

"Sure, no problem." Belle never suspected her dear Auntie Tessa would lie.

A minute later, I had Hiro's cell number. I stared at the digits glowing on my screen. My thumb hovered over the call button. Then I pressed it and… Hiro was at my place in twenty minutes.

The knock came just as the kettle clicked off. I hadn't realized I'd been holding my breath until the whistling sound startled it loose. The sunrise slanted through the kitchen window, spilling gold across the countertops. I smoothed my hair and wiped a faint streak of marinara from my sleeve.

When I opened the door, Hiro Tanaka stood there, all quiet presence and pressed lines. The early light cut across his shoulders, painting him in pale gold and long shadows. He looked every bit the man I'd first mistaken for made-of-stone—and then some.

Ellie saw him first. She squealed, darted forward, and launched herself into his arms. He caught her easily, one hand steady at her back, the other bracing on the doorframe.

"Daddy!" she chirped, nuzzling into his neck.

Her father kissed the top of her head, then looked over her curls to me. "How were they?"

I glanced at Sam, who was hovering behind me with a guilty kind of stillness. The kid and I shared a look. It was a secret understanding between the exhausted and the complicit.

"They were fine," I said.

Hiro's brow arched. The corner of his mouth twitched, unconvinced.

Ellie wriggled in his arms. "I didn't like Ms. Tessa's spaghetti."

Hiro's gaze slid back to me.

Before I could defend my sauce, Sam spoke up. "I handled it. I cleaned up after her."

Hiro sighed—quiet, deep, the kind of sigh that carried both love and weariness. He set Ellie down. Immediately, the little girl turned on the charm: hands clasped, chin tilted, eyes wide and watery.

"Ellie," Hiro said, calm but firm, "tell me about your behavior."

She twisted a lock of her hair around her finger. "I… maybe spilled the spaghetti a little."

"A little?"

Her mouth tugged sideways. "A lot."

"Was that good behavior?"

She shook her head, curls bouncing. "No."

Hiro crouched to her level, tone steady as breath. "What should your consequence be?"

Ellie's lip trembled. "No screen time… no snack… and I'll stay in my room forever."

The first real smile cracked Hiro's face, soft and unguarded. "That's a little harsh. I'll take the no screen time."

Then he looked to me. "And what else do we say, Ellie?"

She turned, eyes suddenly bright with remorse. "I'm sorry, Ms. Tessa," she whispered, and before I could respond, she wrapped her arms around my legs.

My heart softened despite itself. "Thank you, sweetheart. All forgiven."

"Go get your things," Hiro said. Ellie dashed off down the hall, Sam close on her heels.

Hiro stopped Sam with a hand on his shoulder. "I appreciate you helping Ms. Tessa," he said, lowering his voice. "That was kind. But your sister made the mess. We have to let her learn to clean up after herself, okay?"

Sam nodded, cheeks pink with embarrassment. "Yes, sir."

Hiro ruffled his hair, the gesture both affectionate and grounding. "Thank you, though. You did the right thing helping Ms. Tessa."

Sam smiled faintly and hurried after his sister.

For a moment, the house was quiet again. Just the kettle cooling and the faint patter of children's feet fading down the hall.

I looked at Hiro, truly looked at him, and felt something inside me shift. I'd misjudged him. His patience wasn't detachment. It was discipline wrapped in compassion, quiet but unwavering.

"I'm guessing she didn't ask for an overnight sitting job?"

She? Oh, Marianne. I bit my tongue, then realized I didn't owe her that much loyalty, so I spilled the deets. "She texted to say she was tipsy and didn't want to drive."

"She probably planned to drink before she even dropped them off. I'm sorry you got caught in the middle."

I didn't bother to tell him I'd thought the same thing. He knew her better. He'd loved her. Was that what love looked like when it was used to disappointment?

Hiro turned back to me. "I'm sorry about last night, Tessa. Marianne shouldn't have done that to you."

I shook my head. "It's not your fault. You can't take responsibility—or consequences—for her choices."

Something flickered in his eyes then, something between gratitude and surprise. He smiled—small but real.

"If anything like that ever happens again… please don't hesitate to call me. That is—if you're willing to watch them again after last night."

"I'd watch them again. Especially if you're the one who needs a break."

I let out a little gasp the moment the words left my mouth. There was the slightest intake of air that slipped in-between Hiro Tanaka's parted lips. It felt like he'd just stolen my breath. For a moment, the air shifted between us—something warm and quiet threading through the morning light. His eyes softened, but he didn't step closer.

"Thank you," he said simply.

The kids reappeared, backpacks slung over small shoulders, Ellie clutching her stuffed rabbit like armor.

As they headed for the door, I called after him, "You have my number now, if you need it."

Hiro turned, that half-smile back on his lips. "Yes."

And then they were gone. They left behind a morning that was suddenly too still, too empty. I stood in the doorway, hand still on the knob, pretending I wasn't hoping he'd find a reason to use my number.

CHAPTER TWENTY

The Stillwater Tavern was half full, half lit, and wholly alive. Warm light pooled over the worn bar top, catching on the glassware and the golden heads of beer like little halos. Someone had queued up a Cindy Lauper song on the jukebox, and the whole room hummed with the same wistful rhythm.

Our table—the girls' table—sat tucked in the corner beneath a framed photo of the old Stillwater Springs Fair. "No boys allowed," Lana had declared when she made the reservation, wagging her finger at the bartender like she owned the place.

So naturally, when a familiar cluster of men strolled past the window outside—Bo, Theo, Zach, and a couple of the other men from town—we all turned to look.

Lana's grin went dreamy. "There's my man."

Celia laughed, eyes tracking Bo's broad shoulders as he tipped his head in greeting through the glass. "Mine too."

They both sighed—synchronized and unapologetic—as the men kept walking, hands tucked in their pockets, bound for Layla's Sports Bar across the street. Layla's place wasn't fancy, but it didn't need to be. Its brick façade glowed with the warm, amber light of packed Friday nights, jerseys framed on the walls like stained glass for the church of has-been athletes and weekend warriors.

Layla herself had been a legend here long before she ever hung her name over that door. The girl who'd taken Stillwater High all the way to state. The one who'd earned the full ride, the WNBA draft pick, the dream everyone in town had lived vicariously through. And then, pregnant in her second season, she'd stepped off the court without a flicker of regret. Came straight home, raised her son, and built a bar where men could relive their glory days while she topped off their mugs and trash-talked their fantasy leagues with the authority of someone who'd actually dominated a court.

Aside from Celia and her books, Layla was the other famous woman from Stillwater. And she wore it like everything else—casually, shoulders loose, grin wide, as if fame was just another thing she could dribble behind her back.

Belle rolled her eyes at Celia, who was ogling her father's butt. "You two are hopeless."

Celia reached across the table, nudging Belle's glass toward her. "What about your date the other night?"

Belle groaned. "It was meh."

"Meh?" Lana repeated, mock-offended. "That's not a review—it's a sound effect."

Belle shrugged, unbothered. "He was nice enough, just… not it."

"What's *it*?" I asked, swirling my wine.

Belle smiled faintly, gaze drifting toward the window where the guys were disappearing into Layla's. "Kind. Compassionate. Loyal. Someone who makes me feel safe. I don't think that's too much to ask."

Before any of us could reply, her phone buzzed. She looked down at the screen, and her expression softened instantly.

"Excuse me a sec," she murmured, standing. "It's

Zach. Just texting to say thanks for helping me today."

The moment she stepped away, the table hummed with knowing energy.

Lana arched a brow. "Helping her today, huh?"

Celia's grin was conspiratorial. "Those two are a slow burn if I've ever seen one."

Both Lana and I raised a brow at her.

"What? A mom can't want a great romance for her son? Belle's a good girl… despite her mother." That last part was said under her breath only loud enough for me and Lana to hear.

I smiled into my wineglass, letting their chatter wash over me. The gentle teasing, the warmth, the shorthand of women who'd known each other half their lives—it was all so familiar. So safe.

"God, it's nice to sit through a meal without wiping someone's nose or butt," Miranda from the writing club women said, and the table erupted in laughter.

"Or picking up after anyone," said her sister Carmen. "Honestly, I've been divorced for five years now and I still flinch when I see a laundry pile."

"Or the anxiety," Celia said softly. "The constant worry of did I do enough, say enough, love enough?

And now... you send them off to school and just pray that every kid there is okay too."

A murmur of agreement rippled through the table.

I sat back, hands wrapped around my glass, feeling their words settle in my chest. I'd never thought of parenting that way—how it stretched beyond your own child, into the wide, unpredictable world. How your heart wasn't just walking outside your body but sitting in classrooms beside other hearts, all of them fragile, all of them breakable.

I took a slow breath, my practiced kind—the kind that looked like serenity from the outside. But inside, something was moving. Shifting.

The night had that sweet, drowsy glow that comes after the second round of drinks and the third round of laughter. Our table was a small island of warmth and noise in the dim hum of the tavern. Outside, rain threatened, lazy droplets drifting past the window like second thoughts.

"Honestly," one of the writing club women said, shaking her head, "I'm just grateful we got our kids through in one piece. The world feels... different now. Meaner, somehow."

Another woman sighed, nodding. "And more expensive. My daughter's rent is more than our first mortgage. I told her to marry rich, and she said, 'Mom, I'm just trying to date someone emotionally stable.'"

That earned a chorus of *damns*.

"I can't even imagine raising a kid in this world," Celia said. "Social media, AI, all that divisiveness online—it's like the whole planet's arguing in the world's longest group chat."

Lana raised her glass. "Here's to surviving parenthood before TikTok."

We clinked glasses, the sound bright and hollow, like wind chimes before a storm.

They kept going, voices overlapping, warm and wistful. About how they'd made it through the years of carpools and curfews, the late-night ER visits and college drop-offs. About how they'd done their time and earned their freedom.

I listened, smiling where I should, nodding where it fit. But under the practiced serenity, a small ache pressed in.

Freedom. That was the word they kept circling. And here I was, about to give mine away willingly.

Lana turned to me, eyes bright, a little wine-warm. "Aren't you glad you never had to go through any of that, Tess? You get to enjoy your life in peace now."

I opened my mouth, but she was already rolling on, laughing. "And with no more excuses from us, that means we can finally go out, stay out, travel! We need a girls' trip. A cruise this summer!"

A cruise. In summer. By then… I'd have a baby.

I bit my lip, caught between the lie of my smile and the truth pressing just behind my ribs. I could already see it—Lana in a sun hat, Celia with a cocktail, me pretending to relax while worrying about nap schedules and diaper bags.

Celia leaned in, squinting at me like she could read my thoughts. "Oh my God. It's the guy, isn't it? That's why you're hesitating. You don't want to leave your new man."

Okay, this had gone on long enough. It was time to come clean. "I don't—there's no—"

But before I could get the words out, the door opened. And there he was.

Hiro Tanaka stepped inside, the damp night trailing him like a shadow, his coat still dusted with droplets. He looked exactly the same as the last time I'd seen him—broad shoulders, quiet steadiness—but under the tavern lights, there was something almost warm about him.

Celia and Lana followed my gaze, their voices dropping in tandem.

"Is that him?"

"No," I said, way too quick and defensive. "I mean —yes. But no. He's—"

Before I could finish the sentence, Belle slid back into her seat, her phone tucked into her pocket. "What'd I miss?"

Celia smirked. "Aunt Tessa has a new boyfriend."

Belle followed their gazes toward a booth near the bar where Hiro was pulling papers out of his leather satchel. When her eyes landed on Hiro, her brows shot up. "Wait, Professor Tanaka? Is that why you wanted his phone number?"

Every pair of eyes turned to me.

From across the room, Hiro looked up—and caught my gaze.

The breath I'd just taken refused to leave my lungs.

I wasn't sure if I wanted to disappear… or wave.

"He's cute."

"He's a professor."

"How's he in bed?"

I choked on my wine. "We haven't—"

I stopped talking, but the damage was already done. Either I confessed the truth—that I wasn't dating Hiro Tanaka, that there was no secret romance, that the only thing I was incubating was the hope of becoming a mother—or I let them keep believing I was finally getting some.

The truth would invite the wrong kind of reaction. Pity. Concern. Those annoying, careful looks people gave me after Darnell died, as though I might crumble if they breathed too hard in my direction.

I'd hated losing my husband. But I'd been

prepared for it. We'd soaked up every moment that we could and lived it to the fullest with no regrets. Well, except one.

I couldn't stand facing those looks again. Especially with that single regret hanging over my head. So I did the only thing that made sense after two glasses of merlot and twenty years of pretending to be endlessly composed. I picked up my drink and walked toward Hiro Tanaka with the intention of asking him to break up with me.

Behind me came the catcalls—Lana's two-finger whistle, Celia's mock growl, Belle's laughter sharp enough to cut glass.

"Go get him, Mama!" someone shouted.

I ignored them and focused on the man in the corner booth. He sat alone, the leather briefcase open beside him, papers spread in tidy chaos. A pencil rested behind his ear, his beer more than half full. He looked tired in the way good men did—worn around the eyes but still upright. Steady. I had the strangest urge to smooth the crease between his brows with my thumb.

When he looked up and saw me approaching, he blinked in surprise—and then smiled. It was small, almost shy, but it reached his eyes.

"Tessa," he said, voice low, that calm baritone that always sounded like control personified.

"I need a favor," I blurted out.

Hiro blinked once, then said evenly, "Name it."

"I need you to break up with me."

That startled a laugh out of him. "I wasn't aware we were together."

I gestured to the empty seat across from him. He nodded, inviting me to sit.

"Okay," he said, amusement still playing at the corners of his mouth. "Explain."

I took a breath, clasped my hands on the table like I was about to deliver bad news. "You met Lila."

"I did," he said carefully.

"She's pregnant," I went on.

His expression didn't change, except for the faint arch of a brow. "It's never polite for a man to assume such a thing."

Despite myself, I smiled. "You're right. But this time, you'd be correct."

Hiro gave a quiet hum of acknowledgment, waiting.

"Marianne's helping me adopt her baby. The paperwork's in motion."

His brows lifted, but it wasn't pity I saw there.

Just… understanding. The kind that didn't ask questions.

"I'm not ready to tell my friends, but I've been dodging plans and missing girls' nights, and somehow, they've decided I must be dating someone."

"And they think that someone is me."

"Yes," I sighed. "Apparently, getting your number from Belle was a mistake."

Hiro's upper lip twitched. Then the lower one tugged into a smirk. I was so focused on his mouth that I missed what he said and had to replay the sounds in my head to try and determine their meaning.

"So what exactly did I do?"

"Beg pardon?"

"Well," he said, leaning back slightly, that infuriating half-smile deepening, "if we're ending things, I'd at least like to know what I did wrong."

I blinked at him, caught off guard by his humor. "Good point. You're totally my type. Smart, kind, compassionate, great with kids…"

My words trailed off as I realized what I'd just admitted out loud.

Hiro was full-on smiling now, the kind of smile that made it hard to remember the plan or even the reason I'd come over in the first place.

I thought of Belle's words earlier: *Kind. Compassionate. Loyal. Makes me feel safe.*

God help me, Hiro Tanaka was all of those things. Suddenly, this fake breakup didn't feel nearly as hypothetical as I'd intended.

"It has to be my kids then."

"Your kids?"

"They're a handful."

"They're not that bad."

Hiro raised one of those dark, skeptical eyebrows. If I wasn't careful, this man would unravel me with just that look. He waited, patient as ever, and for reasons I didn't fully understand, the quiet between us turned into a confession booth.

"I lied to my husband," I said softly.

His smile faded, not in judgment but in careful attention.

"He didn't want children," I continued, tracing the rim of my near empty wine glass. "Not because he hated kids. He was… good with them, actually. He just didn't want any of his own. And I—" I gave a small, humorless laugh. "I said I didn't need to be a mom. That love would be enough."

I wrinkled my nose, realizing how naïve that sounded even now.

"I told myself I could live without that kind of

love because I had him. And for a while, it worked. But now…"

Hiro leaned forward, his expression softening, his pencil still tucked behind his ear like he'd forgotten it was there. "You're divorced?"

I shook my head. "No. He passed away."

"I'm sorry." There was no pity in his tone, just compassion. It sat still beside me instead of rushing to fill the silence.

"Now that he's gone," I said, my voice thinner than I meant it to be, "all those old feelings have come back. I want to share my heart again. My home. My life. With someone new. With a child. I want to go through all the things my friends complain about—the good, the bad, and the ugly. The spaghetti on the walls."

That last line made him laugh. The sound rolled through him, low and warm, like the soft crack of a log in a fireplace.

"Then maybe we shouldn't break up."

I blinked. "Beg your pardon?"

"If we're already dating in everyone's minds, we might as well keep it that way. At least until you're ready to tell your friends the truth."

My pulse did a strange little yoga pose of its own —twisting, stretching, refusing to settle. I searched

Hiro's face for the joke, the tease, but he wasn't smirking. He was just... looking at me. Steady. Thoughtful. That maddening, measured calm that made me want to both exhale and shake him.

"Fake dating," I repeated, as if saying it out loud might make it less absurd.

He lifted his beer, eyes glinting with something I couldn't quite name. "Seems less complicated than a fake breakup."

I should've said no. I should've laughed it off, thanked him, and walked back to my friends and their wine and their easy certainty about the world.

Instead, I found myself smiling—widely, help-lessly. "You're one of the good ones, aren't you?"

"That's up for debate."

Who would debate that? Then I realized exactly who. His ex-wife. The woman I was still depending on to push through my paperwork with Child Social Services. Maybe this wasn't a good idea after all.

Then again, Marianne didn't have to know.

CHAPTER TWENTY-TWO

I floated home that night. Half of me was buoyed by laughter, the other half was a bubbling, effervescent feeling I hadn't felt in years. My girlfriends thought I was dating a hot guy. Said hot guy had let me hide out beside him in the corner booth, grading papers in companionable silence while music hummed low between us. We didn't talk much—just shared the quiet, that way when two people understand that stillness can be intimate.

When I saw my girls starting to get restless—Lana chair dancing, Celia nodding off—I knew it was only a matter of time before they came over and grilled us both. So I'd thanked Hiro for the refuge, laying a hand on his arm in gratitude. I hadn't meant to notice how solid he was beneath that Henley, but I did. Every muscle under my palm felt like restraint personified.

He gave me the medium smile. I wasn't sure when I had started cataloging the sizes of Hiro Tanaka's smiles like weather patterns I needed to predict. But I had.

There was the small one he'd cautiously passed on after our disastrous first meeting. That one was absentminded, almost academic. A polite upward tilt of the mouth, the kind he probably offered to students after a thoughtful question or a half-decent essay. It held acknowledgment but not much emotion, like a bookmark slipped between pages: *I might come back to this later.*

Then there was his medium smile. He'd given it to me a few times tonight. This one reached his eyes. Softened them. It said, *I see you. I'm glad you're here.* It was a small, quiet gift I'd wanted to rewrap, only to slowly peel off the layers again and again.

And then there was the big smile. I'd only seen it twice—both times directed at his children, bursting out of him like sunlight after a storm. It transformed him, lit him from the inside. The big smile said, *You are my joy. You are my heart walking around outside my body.* Somewhere along the way, without my permission, I'd started wanting that smile. Wanting to be someone who drew that kind of warmth from this man.

But not tonight. Tonight, the medium smile was enough. Tonight, I didn't trust myself with anything bigger.

By the time I got Celia bundled off with Bo—who'd appeared like some kind of broad-shouldered guardian angel—and watched Lana melt into Theo's arms, all their questions about Hiro had vanished into the night air.

The drive home was short. I still had that faint aftertaste of happiness—warm, fizzy, fragile. Until I saw the old, dented truck in my driveway and heard the shouting.

My pulse stuttered. I didn't run exactly, but my steps quickened as I pushed through the front door.

Inside, the calm of my sanctuary had been broken wide open. Lila stood in the middle of the living room, her face blotched red, her hands trembling. Across from her, a man and a woman—gray-haired, severe, dressed in the kind of Sunday best that reeked of righteousness—loomed like judges.

"You will not keep that child," the woman spat, voice quivering with venom. "We've spoken to Pastor Reynolds, and he's found a nice family who'll take that bastard baby off our hands. You'll come home, and you'll repent."

Lila's voice came out small but steady. "I'm not coming home."

"You don't get to make that decision," her father snapped. His tie was crooked, his eyes sharp with indignation. "You are still a minor."

That was enough for me.

"Not in my house," I said, stepping fully into the room.

All three of them turned toward me. The mother's gaze darted from the high heels on my feet to my strappy dress. Her lip curled as though she'd caught me in some great sin.

"This is a private matter," she said stiffly. "Between us and our daughter."

"Correction," I said, voice smooth as glass, even though my heart pounded beneath it. "You kicked her out. That means she's not your responsibility anymore. She's under the care of Child Protective Services now. If you'd like, I can call her representative and have an officer here in five minutes to confirm that."

The father bristled. "We'll be speaking to our attorney."

"Wonderful," I said sweetly. "Be sure to tell him

that you trespassed, harassed a minor, and verbally assaulted a CPS ward. I'm sure they'll love that."

Color drained from his face, replaced by a cold, burning anger.

Lila's mother turned her fury back on her daughter. "You shame us," she hissed. "And you"—she aimed a trembling finger at me—"you're a demonic teacher, filling her head with lies. Yoga is the devil's work."

"Well," I said evenly, "I prefer deep breathing to exorcisms, but to each their own."

The woman's gasp was almost satisfying. They left in a huff of indignation and holy fury, the door slamming so hard the walls shuddered with relief at their exit.

Lila stood frozen, her breath coming in little gasps, her eyes bright with unshed tears. Then, in a small, shaking voice, she said, "I'll get my stuff and go. I should've known they'd find me here. I'm so sorry they brought that into your house."

"You're not going anywhere, sweetheart."

Her chin trembled. "You mean... until I have the baby. Until you—" She swallowed hard. "Until you get your baby."

"No, Lila. I mean as long as you need a place. Period."

Her eyes flicked up to mine, searching for the catch, the expiration date in my tone.

"You're safe here, Lila. This is your home for as long as you want it."

But even as she nodded, I could see it—the disbelief flickering behind her exhaustion. She didn't believe she could belong anywhere. And though I told myself peace was something you could create, right then, standing in my quiet living room, I realized peace might also be something you had to fight for.

I was willing to fight for this baby. I was willing to fight for Lila. Was it crazy to fight for both of them? Was I taking on too much?

Watching Lila walk away, watching her hand on her belly, I realized it wasn't. I wanted them both. I wanted to take care of them both.

It was fine that Lila didn't believe me; I'd show her. It was fine that my friends would think I was crazy. To me, it felt like the rightest thing in the world.

CHAPTER TWENTY-THREE

I was rolling out a mat when Lana breezed through the door. She was in full-on counselor mode, still in her designer jacket, yoga pants and heels, her hair escaping its bun like it had been negotiating a settlement with gravity all day.

"Lord, give me flexibility or give me wine," she sighed, dropping her bag by the wall.

"I can give you reclining butterfly pose." I smiled, reaching for the music controls.

"I'll take it."

Lana kicked off her heels with the kind of theatrical groan that belonged on a stage, not a yoga studio floor. One shoe skittered across the hardwood; the other simply gave up and flopped on its side. Then she folded herself down into Butterfly Pose with all the grace of a wilted fern.

I couldn't help it—I laughed. I loved this side of my bestie, the side that didn't take herself seriously. This side of Lana would listen about Lila and the baby.

But while she opened her hips in butterfly pose, I couldn't open my mouth just yet. Women from the community were filtering in—mats unrolling, chatter softening into anticipation. Evening classes were my favorite: the day's noise settled, and all that was left was breath and body, the slow unraveling of everything we'd held too tightly.

I was just about to begin when the door swung open. Marianne barged in. Late, flustered, and—of course—on her phone.

Her voice carried across the quiet like a pebble dropped in still water. "I am trying to prioritize self-care. You should try it sometime."

A few of the women exchanged looks, the kind that hovered between amusement—because they wanted to hear the gossip—and irritation—because they wanted to claim their peace in this quiet space.

Marianne caught their eyes, grimaced, and mouthed, *Sorry* before hurrying to the back of the room. She tossed her bag down, rolled out a mat, and ended the call with a tight, "Fine. I'll see you later."

The silence she left behind was heavy enough to cut. I took a slow inhale, trying to coax my own breath back into rhythm. Two of my worlds—Lana and Marianne—colliding in one small, incense-scented room. Wonderful.

"Let's start in mountain pose. Feet grounded, heart open."

It took me a few minutes to find the center of the class again, to let the rhythm of cueing and breathing override the buzzing in my chest. But soon the energy shifted and softened. Muscles lengthened, shoulders lowered, and the hum of human stillness filled the space.

By the time we moved into Savasana, the tension had melted into the peace we all sought. The lights dimmed, breaths deepened, and for ten blessed minutes, the world outside stopped spinning. When the final bell chimed, the women rose slowly, that post-yoga glow settling over them like candlelight. A few came up to thank me, smiling, loose, and radiant.

Lana stretched her arms overhead. "I needed that. I'm staying for tea, by the way," she said, already heading for the changing room. "You, me, girl talk. I want to know more about this new Hiro of yours."

My gaze slid to Marianne, but she was just coming out of the Savasana.

Still, I hesitated. I couldn't take Lana back to my place. Lila was home. But I couldn't keep hiding the truth from my best friend. Tonight, I'd have to tell her everything.

"Tea sounds good."

"I'll go change and be right back."

As Lana disappeared into the back, Marianne approached. Her phone was already back in her hand, the glow of the screen lighting her frown. She didn't look at peace. If anything, she looked like she'd come out more tangled than she went in.

"Everything okay?" I asked, careful and kind. I realized I was more worried about her kids and her ex than I was about her.

"Just my ex being inflexible. He's at my place with the kids, and I'm running late because I—God forbid —took a little time for myself."

I nodded, murmuring something sympathetic, though my stomach had started to knot.

Marianne looked up, her expression suddenly hopeful. "Would you mind if Hiro just dropped the kids here for me?"

My mind immediately painted the picture: Hiro walking through the door, Lana walking out of the changing room. Was the universe trying to play some kind of cosmic prank on me?

"I actually have plans," I said quickly.

Marianne's face fell, the disappointment plain. "Oh. I just thought… after everything, you might be able to help me out. I did spend a lot of extra hours pushing that paperwork through for you."

The words landed like pebbles in my gut. Out of the corner of my eye, I saw Lana heading our way, her purse slung over her shoulder and that mischievous grin already forming.

Marianne's phone pinged again. She glanced down and muttered, "God, Hiro, I said I was coming. Jeez, my ex-husband can be such a tool sometimes."

Lana froze mid-step. "Hiro?" She looked between us. Then she jabbed a finger at me —dead center at my chest. "Your Hiro?"

I took a slow, deliberate breath. In through the nose. Out through the mouth. *Stay grounded. Stay calm.* Two women. One misunderstanding. A room still scented with lavender and potential chaos. What could go wrong?

"Lana, this is Marianne—Hiro's ex-wife."

Lana's jaw dropped so far I half expected it to hit the mat.

"Lana, would you excuse me and Marianne for just a minute?"

Lana blinked between us, clearly dying for the gossip but too polite—or maybe too stunned—to push it. "Sure. I'll… go wait outside."

The moment the door swung shut behind her, Marianne rounded on me.

"You've got to be kidding me." Her voice was low but sharp enough to cut. "Some friend you are. You're sleeping with my husband?"

My mouth actually fell open. "What? I'm not sleeping with Hiro," I said, a little too fast, a little too defensive. "I'm not even dating him."

Marianne's brows arched high. "Really?"

"Yes, really." I pressed a hand to my chest, trying to find my calm center, but it kept slipping like a bar of soap. "Look, I didn't tell my friends I was adopting, and I kept blowing them off when I was with you or Lila, so they assumed I was seeing someone. I let them because it seemed easier than having everyone argue with me about my life choices."

"Wow." Marianne's expression softened, her mouth quirking to the side. "You've got lame friends.

Personally, I'm not one to judge. Pot meet kettle, and all."

I blinked at her, thrown by the bluntness—and, weirdly, the kindness under it. If that was kindness?

Before I could form a response, Marianne tilted her head, curiosity brightening her eyes. "Okay, but how did Hiro get dragged into all this?"

"I needed his number when I was babysitting the kids and asked a friend for it. Then everyone just… assumed."

Marianne grinned, the earlier anger evaporating as fast as it had come. "Oh, that's rich. Hiro has zero game, even before we started dating. He spends his nights without the kids grading papers and completely oblivious to the rest of the world. Which is why it pisses me off when he won't take the kids when I need a night out. It's not like he has anything else to do."

I opened my mouth. Closed it. Then opened it again.

"Relax, Tess. I won't tell anyone you're having a torrid imaginary affair with my ex-husband."

"Appreciated." My tone was flat.

Marianne winked. Then a bundle of energy burst in through the doors of the yoga studio. Ellie hurtled herself at her mom.

"Mommy! Daddy took us for ice cream! It was so yummy even though it didn't have sprinkles!"

Marianne's lips puckered into a theatrical pout. "No sprinkles? Oh, sweetheart, that's terrible. I bet the ice cream Mommy gets you is better, isn't it? The real kind with brownie chunks and cookie dough and rainbow sprinkles?"

Ellie nodded enthusiastically, curls bouncing. "I love Mommy's ice cream!"

Marianne's pout turned into a wide smile. "And who do you love the most?"

"Mommy!"

"How much?"

Ellie stretched her little arms as wide as they would go. "This much!"

Marianne laughed and swept her into a hug so tight Ellie squealed. "That's my girl."

The whole thing happened in seconds, bright and sugary on the surface—but something in my stomach went sour as I watched. I knew what this was. It was manipulation disguised as affection.

Hiro stood just inside the doorway, Sam by his side. He took in the scene quietly—Marianne clutching Ellie, Ellie glowing under the weight of her mother's approval—and then his eyes met mine.

A silent recognition passed between us.

Marianne straightened, still holding Ellie's hand. "You just show up after taking my kids out for ice cream?"

"It wasn't ice cream; it was fruit sorbet," he said calmly.

"That's my thing," Marianne snapped, her voice rising. "I'm the one who takes them for ice cream. You know that. You're always doing this; trying to one-up me, trying to make them like you more so I'm the bad guy when I say no."

Hiro's expression didn't shift, though I saw the faintest flicker of hurt behind his calm. "That's not what I'm doing."

"It's not just ice cream when you're stealing the little things I have left. You get to be the fun parent. I get to be the one who makes them eat vegetables and do homework and go to bed on time. So excuse me if I don't appreciate you taking my one good thing."

He raised an eyebrow but didn't argue. I somehow doubted that responsible bent with the veggies and homework was Marianne's style of parenting. Marianne kept going.

Ellie was staring up at them, confusion tightening her little face. Sam shifted uncomfortably, shoulders hunching. The air in the studio thickened, every ounce of peace I'd built evaporating into the tension between them.

I bent down toward Sam, who was hovering close to his father, eyes darting anxiously. "Hey, you two want to come see my koi pond while your parents finish talking?"

Sam nodded quickly, grateful for the escape. Ellie, never one to refuse attention, clapped her hands. "Fishies!"

"Fishies," I confirmed, giving her an encouraging smile.

The three of us slipped outside. Sam slipped his small hand into mine. Ellie darted ahead, a whirl of pink and chatter.

Lana, who had been waiting on the porch, raised a perfectly arched eyebrow as we passed. From inside, Marianne's voice carried—sharp, accusatory, and rising in volume.

Lana tilted her head toward the noise. "What exactly have you gotten yourself into, Tessie?"

I watched Ellie lean over the pond's edge. Sam reached out to grab the back of her jacket, his protectiveness automatic.

"I honestly," I said softly, "have no idea."

CHAPTER TWENTY-FOUR

The koi moved lazily beneath the surface, their bright scales glinting gold and white in the fading light. Ellie leaned so close her breath rippled the water. She giggled each time a fish surfaced for air. Sam crouched beside her, silent, tracing little ripples with one careful finger.

Behind us, Marianne's voice still carried—sharp, rising, jagged as cracked glass. I tried to tune her out. Not just for myself, but for the benefit of her young, impressionable children. I focused instead on the soft plop of water, the slow ballet of orange fins, the first shy stars winking alive over the lake.

For a moment, it worked. Ellie's laughter sparkled across the pond, louder than her mother's anger. Sam's shoulders loosened. Even the koi seemed to move with a gentler rhythm, like they, too, hoped the world would settle.

Lana shifted her weight beside me. She'd followed us over to the pond after Marianne started in on Hiro again. She'd kept quiet, watching the children, watching me. I could practically feel the buzz of her thoughts, the argument forming behind her teeth, the judgment she was trying—not very successfully—to swallow.

Her presence felt like standing next to a storm cloud wearing perfume. She didn't say a word, but that never stopped me from hearing her. I knew that stance—arms folded just loosely enough to look casual, chin slightly lifted, eyes sharp as a cross-examination. She was worried. She was irritated. She was dying to demand why I was entangled in another family's chaos. Dying to tell me I was too kind, too hopeful, too easily bruised.

But she didn't speak. And I also knew why.

Lana and her ex-husband had never once argued in front of their daughters. Not even during the divorce. They'd kept their battles quiet, contained, behind closed doors. The girls still felt the tension, of course. Children always do. But Lana believed in shielding them from the worst of it. She still did.

So she wouldn't pick a fight with me. Not while

little eyes were watching. Not while someone else's family was unraveling on the other side of the retreat's door.

I had a reprieve. Albeit a temporary one, the kind held together by koi ponds and bedtime hour and the fragile hush of children clawing at normalcy. But I could feel Lana's gaze, steady as a hand on the back of my neck.

Concern. Judgment. Love. All tangled up. The same mixture she'd been giving me since we were teenagers.

I drew in a breath, slow and measured, as though serenity could be inhaled on command. All at once, the world went still. Even the koi froze mid-swim. The studio door opened, then slammed hard enough to rattle the wind chime.

Marianne stormed past us, keys clutched tightly in one hand. "I just need space," she said, her voice trembling with fury. "You're crowding me. I can't breathe when you do this."

And then she was gone—tires spitting gravel as her car disappeared down the drive. For a moment, none of us moved. The silence that followed was heavy, unnatural. Then Ellie's lower lip trembled.

"Daddy made Mommy sad again," she sobbed,

her little hands balled into fists. "She's running away!"

Hiro stepped forward, calm as a tide rolling in. He crouched low, scooping Ellie up even as she flailed against his chest.

"Hey, hey," he murmured, his voice soft but steady. "Mommy's not running away, sweetheart. Mommy just needs a time-out. Grown-ups need those sometimes."

Ellie sniffled, hiccupping into his shirt.

He smoothed her hair back, his patience so deliberate it almost felt like prayer. "Mommy loves you. She loves Sam, too. We were just talking about grown-up things. None of this is your fault, okay?"

And just like that, something in me broke open. This was a quieter breaking, like a shell cracking to reveal something tender and luminous inside. Watching him with his children—so soft, so sure, so heartbreakingly gentle—it was impossible not to feel it.

I'd misjudged him.

I'd misjudged all of them.

Those times I'd seen Ellie melting down in public and assumed Hiro lacked control. Those moments in the grocery store or the parking lot when he'd stood so still, so calm, so maddeningly firm while his daughter shrieked—I'd thought he was part of the chaos.

But he never had been. He was the still point. The anchor. The eye of the storm. That storm had a name.

Marianne was at the center of it. She was every flare of distress in Ellie's small body, every tight coil of anxiety in Sam's shoulders. The whirlwind that spun around them, tossing their little hearts back and forth until they didn't know where to land.

But Hiro—God, Hiro—he was the refuge. The calm. The one who stood in the wreckage and tried, every single time, to make sense of the emotional debris for his kids. To protect them even when he couldn't protect himself.

My breath caught in my throat, too full, too tight. I pressed a hand to my chest like I could hold myself steady the way he held his daughter. I'd thought I understood patience. I taught serenity for a living. Whatever lived in Hiro Tanaka… it was something else entirely. Something I couldn't help but want to be near.

Hiro shifted his gaze to Sam, whose small shoulders were drawn tight as wire. "You hear me, buddy? You don't have to worry about adult stuff. You've just got to do your kid work—school, chores, being good, remembering that your parents love you always. That's your job."

Sam nodded mutely, his chin quivering. Ellie clung tighter to her father's neck.

Beside me, Lana let out a slow exhale. "Well," she whispered, squeezing my hand. "You found a good one, Tess. Too bad he comes with a certified crazy ex."

I shot her a warning look, but she was already backing toward the parking lot. "We'll talk later," she said softly, giving my arm one last squeeze before slipping away.

When she was gone, I turned back to Hiro. He was still crouched, his daughter's arms looped around his neck, his son standing close by like a small, solemn shadow.

"Can I help?"

Hiro glanced up, weary but composed. "No. This isn't your responsibility."

"I know." I hesitated, my voice gentling. "But if I can help, I want to. You, Sam, and Ellie—you're my friends. And a friend's job is to show up when they need help."

Hiro studied me for a long moment, the air between us threaded with unspoken things. "I have a lecture in twenty minutes," he said. "I can't cancel it."

"Then go," I told him. "I'll keep the kids. It's no trouble."

Hiro hesitated, his expression softening, that quiet composure of his finally cracking into something more human—something grateful.

"I'll be right back after class," he promised.

"Take your time," I said. "Maybe even a few minutes for yourself."

He gave a small, incredulous laugh at that—like the idea of a break had never occurred to him.

Then he kissed Ellie's forehead, ruffled Sam's hair, and looked at me again. For a fleeting heartbeat, the gratitude in his eyes made my pulse skip.

And just like that, he was gone—leaving behind the echo of his calm and the faintest trace of warmth that lingered long after his car door closed.

CHAPTER TWENTY-FIVE

By the time we got home, the storm inside all of us had softened into quiet. The house was dim, hushed in that way that only comes after too much emotion and too little sleep.

I made a pot of chamomile tea. One cup with honey for Sam. Another without for Ellie. I didn't need her to get a second wind.

Ellie yawned so hard her tiny shoulders rose with it. She didn't say much for once, just curled onto the couch with her blanket and the mug cupped in both hands. Sam, ever the quiet shadow of his sister's chaos, sipped slowly and kept his eyes on the television.

I put on a nature documentary—something with soft narration and the low hum of ocean waves.

Within minutes, Ellie's lashes fluttered shut. Sam captured her drink before I could. The little guy stayed awake, gaze unfocused, as if watching the screen gave him permission not to think.

"You doing okay, sweetheart?" I asked softly.

He nodded, though he didn't look at me. "I'm fine."

That word again. Fine. So small and brittle.

I wanted to tell him he didn't have to be fine all the time. Already, he carried too much weight for someone so young. I smoothed a hand through his hair and let him have his silence.

I headed for the kitchen and was met with the sound of clinking dishes. Lila was tidying up after dinner. She always tried to make herself useful, like she was afraid to be a burden.

"You don't have to do that."

She glanced up from the sink, sleeves rolled to her elbows. "I want to. You've done so much for me already: the food, the room, taking time off work. It's only fair I help out."

I leaned against the counter, smiling softly. "You being here isn't a burden, Lila. Truly."

She dried her hands, then turned to face me, eyes uncertain. "I was actually wondering if I could maybe… start working at the studio. Just part-time.

Help out with cleaning mats or check-ins or something. I want to contribute."

I crossed the space between us and set a gentle hand on her shoulder. "Your only job right now is to cook that bun in your oven."

Her face shifted—something shuttered, something sad. "I promise I'm not doing anything that will endanger your baby."

Your baby. It didn't sound quite right. It hit like a pebble dropped into still water—small, but the ripples went deep.

"Lila," I said quietly, "are you sure you want to give up this baby?"

She crossed her arms, trying to sound calm but not quite managing it. "I know I can't take care of a baby. I'm trying to do the responsible thing. It's better this way."

I hesitated, watching her. There was bravery in her voice but fear underneath it too. It was an echo of the girl her parents had tried to shame into silence.

"What if you didn't have to do it alone?"

Lila's brows pulled together. "What do you mean?"

"What if you had help? What if we took care of the baby together?"

She blinked at me, her lips parting just slightly. "Are you saying… you want me too?"

Something warm expanded inside my chest. "Yes, sweetheart. I want you too. I think we could make a good family, you and me and this little one. I've got space. And I've got love. Enough for both of you."

Lila's chin trembled before the tears came. Then she threw her arms around me, clinging tightly. I held her there in the quiet kitchen, the tea cooling on the counter, the faint sounds of waves drifting from the living room. For the first time in years, I felt something shift inside me—something that wasn't peace but maybe the beginning of hope.

When Hiro knocked on my door a few hours later, I could tell immediately he hadn't taken my advice to take a moment for himself. He looked like he'd gone ten rounds with exhaustion and still had a few more left to go. His shoulders appeared heavy, his shirt rumpled, his eyes ringed in that deep kind of weariness that seeped past the body and into the soul.

I gestured toward the back porch. "Come sit. I was just making tea."

He hesitated for a moment, like he didn't quite trust himself to slow down, then nodded. We sat on the porch, the night air warm and humming with the soft drone of crickets. The lake caught the faint reflection of the moon, a pale shimmer that pulsed like breath. I poured the tea, the scent of chamomile and mint winding between us like a bridge.

For a while, we didn't speak. Just sat there in the quiet, breathing the same air.

Then Hiro sighed, setting his cup down. "I owe you an apology. For earlier."

"No, you don't. Marianne's behavior isn't yours to answer for."

He nodded slowly, his gaze distant. "Maybe not. But she's still the kids' mother. And I know how she can be."

I wanted to say something kind, something neutral, but what came out instead was the truth. "You handled it beautifully, Hiro. The way you spoke to them… you didn't lose your calm. You didn't shame them. That kind of patience—it's rare."

"I didn't want the divorce, you know."

I scratched at my chest, unsure why I felt an ache there.

"But now… I think it was for the best. We weren't the same people we were when we got married. Parenting changes people. Some for the better. Some for the worse."

The crickets filled the pause that followed. Hiro

leaned back, rubbing the bridge of his nose. "I used to think I could protect the kids from everything; from her temper, from the noise of it all. But I can't. They're going to have to learn to cope with who their mother is. My job now is to give them the tools to do that. But kids find a way to make everything their fault."

I thought of Sam—his small, stoic face, the way his shoulders curled inward as if he were holding up the weight of the world with those fragile bones.

"You're going to be a great mom to Lila's baby."

I swallowed hard, then said my big admission quietly, "I want both of them. Lila and the baby."

Hiro's smile widened, slow and genuine this time. "You really are maternal, aren't you?"

That made me laugh—a real one that caught me by surprise. "If you tell my mom, I'll have to kill you."

We fell into silence again. This one felt different. Warmer. Closer.

He sat just inches away. The porch light traced the strong line of his jaw, the faint stubble shadowing it. His pencil was tucked behind his ear as always, and somehow that tiny, human detail made the ache in my chest deepen. He looked at me then—really looked—and I felt the air shift. His gaze flicked to my mouth. I shouldn't have noticed, but I did.

Oh my God. I wanted to kiss him.

It wasn't just attraction. It wasn't the thrill of attention or the quiet fantasy of those broad shoulders or the professorial calm that made me want to lean in. I wanted to kiss Hiro because he was a good man. Because he knew how to be gentle when the world demanded noise. Because watching him father his children had awakened something inside me I thought I'd buried with Darnell.

I didn't just want to date him. I wanted to build with him. To parent with him. To share the ordinary and the extraordinary.

But then he pulled back. "I think we should break up."

It took me a second to catch up. "I—what?"

"If Marianne thinks we have feelings for each other, she'll turn on you. I don't want that. She'll aim for you just to make me bleed."

I blinked, trying to absorb it. Hiro was trying to protect me, just like he was trying to protect his kids. He was the one drawing Marianne's fire where it could do the least harm. Shielding the world from her chaos, one flare-up at a time.

But who was protecting Hiro Tanaka?

I wanted to kiss him all the more for that. But I didn't. I followed behind him as he collected his kids. I stood on the porch as he buckled them into their safety seats. Then I waved as he drove off into the night.

It was the worst breakup of my life.

CHAPTER TWENTY-SIX

I pulled in front of the community college and put the car in park. The morning sunlight caught on the windshield like gold dust. The air still had that early chill that made everything feel possible.

"Next time, you can take the car," I said. "Save yourself the bus fare."

Lila hesitated. "I don't have a license. My parents never wanted me to learn how to drive." She said it so simply, like she was reciting a fact, but I heard what was underneath—the quiet resignation of someone who'd been told "no" too many times to question it anymore.

I felt that familiar tightening behind my ribs—the one that came whenever I saw just how small her world had been made for her.

"Well, after the baby's born, I'll teach you."

She looked at me, her whole face softening into surprise before blooming into a smile so bright it caught me off guard. "You'd do that?"

"Of course," I said. "It's time you had a little freedom."

She leaned across the console and hugged me, her arms tentative but warm. "Thank you," she whispered before climbing out of the car.

I watched her head toward the entrance, her long braid swinging, that determined little waddle in her step now that the baby was taking up more space. A flicker of pride rose in me—like watching a seedling brave the wind for the first time.

Then I noticed him. Hiro Tanaka stood by the faculty lot, coffee in hand, watching the scene unfold. When our eyes met, his expression softened into something that could only be described as fond amusement. He started toward me, the morning light catching on the faint lines around his eyes.

He leaned down at my window. "Good morning," he said, voice low and smooth as ever.

"Good morning," I returned, trying to sound casual and failing miserably. "How'd you sleep?"

"Very well," he said. "I'm sure it had something to do with the tea."

The corners of my mouth lifted. "Mother Nature makes the potent stuff."

We smiled at each other—too long, too knowingly. The air between us felt warm and fragile, like one deep breath could tip it into something dangerous. Then Hiro straightened, the movement small but final. I caught a flicker of something—regret, maybe—before he stepped back from the car. I shifted into gear, forcing myself to look forward.

"Tessa?"

I turned back. He was still standing there, one hand tucked in his pocket, that half-smile tugging at his mouth.

"Maybe you'll let me return the favor sometime."

"What favor?"

"Babysitting," he said lightly. "After Lila's baby's born. I'm very good with newborns."

My heart stuttered, then tripped over itself entirely. "That's a very generous offer."

Hiro tilted his head. "I'm trying to impress one of the baby's moms."

I couldn't stop the grin that spread across my face. "Lila's a bit young for you, isn't she?"

He smiled wider, the one that reached his eyes.

And that ache in my chest identified itself. I was falling for Professor Tanaka.

"Maybe, after all the CPS paperwork is done—and the baby's born, and everyone's getting some sleep again—the other mom might consider having tea with me?"

I felt the smile curve through me, soft and inevitable. "I thought you broke up with that mom."

Hiro arched an eyebrow. "Maybe I changed my mind."

The ache in my chest migrated low in my stomach. That flutter wasn't nerves exactly but recognition. A spark of something I hadn't felt in years. "I think she'd like that."

Hiro gave a small nod, then stepped back. "Drive safe, Tessa."

As I pulled away, I caught one last glimpse of him in the rearview mirror, standing there with his coffee and that maddeningly calm smile, and realized that for the first time in a long time, I wasn't entirely sure I wanted peace. A little chaos sounded nice.

Fifteen minutes later, I was on the other side of town. The bell above the coffee shop door jingled as I stepped inside, the familiar scent of espresso and cinnamon wrapping around me like comfort itself.

Celia and Lana were already tucked into our usual corner booth, steam curling from their mugs. My drink sat waiting, just the way I liked it—half-caf almond milk latte with a sprinkle of cinnamon on top.

They knew me too well.

"Tessa!" Lana waved me over, eyes bright with gossip. "We were just talking about you."

I smiled, sliding into the booth. "That's never a comforting thing to hear."

Celia leaned forward, her expression full of warmth. "Lana was just telling me about that run-in you had with Hiro's ex at your class. She said you handled it beautifully."

I took a sip of my latte, the warmth spreading through my chest. "Beautifully might be overstating it. I was mostly just trying to keep my breathing even."

Lana snorted. "That's what makes it beautiful, Tess. You're the only person I know who can defuse a situation with deep breathing and eye contact."

Celia chuckled. "Those kids are lucky. They're getting a great stepmom one day."

That word—stepmom—made my nose wrinkle, like the mom on *Bewitched.* Because they were right. If I was going to date Hiro —someday—I would have to care for his kids. The fact was, I already cared for his kids. But I was already taking on two other children. Was I insane to add two adolescents to the mix as well?

Who was I kidding? I wanted it all with Hiro, and the man hadn't even kissed me yet. But I felt as right about him as I had about Darnell.

Lana bumped Celia's shoulder. "Tessa was a great second mom to my girls," she said. "It takes a special kind of patience to handle a Russo."

Celia smiled, her tone turning tender. "And a little insanity."

They laughed, clinking their mugs together. This was it. The moment felt ripe, the kind of space that begged for honesty.

I set my cup down. "Actually, there's something I've been meaning to tell you both."

Two pairs of eyes turned toward me. Expectant. Loving. Safe.

"I was planning to adopt a baby."

The clink of Celia's spoon against her saucer was the only sound. Both her and Lana's eyes went wide, identical in shock.

"But now…" I took a slow breath. "Now I realize I don't just want the baby. I want the baby's mom too.

Her name is Lila—the teen mom carrying her. I want them both to be my family."

If it was possible, their eyes widened more. The silence grew louder. It hummed, thick and brittle.

Celia blinked first. "Tessa…"

Lana leaned forward, voice soft but sharp around the edges. "You must be out of your mind. A baby and a teenager? Tess, what are you thinking?"

Celia reached for my hand. "Sweetheart, you've worked so hard for your peace. Why would you bring that kind of chaos into your life now?"

"And with a new relationship?" Lana added. "A man with two kids and a crazy ex-wife? Tess, come on."

Their words piled one on top of another until I couldn't tell which of them was speaking anymore. All I heard was the disbelief. The fear. The judgment wrapped in concern.

I stared between them, the two women who'd been my anchors through grief, heartbreak, widowhood, everything—and for the first time, I didn't feel anchored at all.

"I knew I was right not to tell you," I said quietly.

Lana's brow furrowed. "Tessa—"

"No." I pushed back from the booth, the chair scraping against the floor louder than I intended. "I have stood beside you both while you made choices I didn't agree with. I showed up. I supported you. Because that's what friends do. But the one time I do something out of character for me—something that's actually in my heart—you can't do the same."

Celia's lips parted. "Tessa, wait—"

But I was already standing, already moving toward the door. My pulse thudded in my ears, my breath shallow and hot in my chest.

The bell jingled again as I pushed through the door into the bright, indifferent sunlight.

I didn't look back.

CHAPTER TWENTY-SEVEN

It had been three days since I'd spoken to either of my best friends. Three long, echoing days filled with texts I didn't answer, glances I pretended not to catch, and the practiced choreography of avoidance.

During class, I kept other students between us like buffers of breath and bodies. During writing group, I'd arranged for the HVAC technician to come at the same time—so I could "supervise."

It was petty. I knew that. But I'd spent my whole life being the adult in the room: the calm one, the caretaker, the defuser. Maybe I just wanted to see what it felt like to sulk for once.

Still, beneath the stubborn silence was a dull ache I couldn't stretch out. Lana and Celia had been my family for decades. But the moment I wanted to build a family of my own, they couldn't see it. Couldn't see me in the role.

The irony wasn't lost on me. I taught people how to release resistance, how to flow with life, and here I was stuck in my own emotional warrior pose, jaw tight, heart trembling.

And then there was Hiro. I missed him too. Though there was no reason for us to talk anymore. Marianne seemed to be co-parenting well—at least for now—and the kids were healthy, busy, and thriving. Which meant I wasn't needed.

That should've been a relief. But the truth was, I'd grown used to the quiet comfort of him. His steadiness. The pencil tucked behind his ear. The way he listened—not to respond but to understand. Every time I passed the tea tin he liked or caught a glimpse of his children's favorite cartoon on the TV guide as I scrolled mindlessly searching for something to occupy the screen, something inside me tugged.

Today, though, there wasn't room for wistfulness. Today, Lila and I were heading to the office to start the adoption paperwork. Or at least to explain that our plans had changed.

Inside CPS, Lila disappeared down the hall to

find a restroom, leaving me alone in the waiting area with the hum of the vending machine and a nervous flutter under my ribs.

That's when I saw him. He was slumped in a chair beside a cluttered desk. There was a blanket draped around his shoulders.

"Sam?" I said softly, tapping on the open door.

His head lifted, eyes lighting up. "Miss Tessa?"

Before I could stop him, he launched himself into my arms. The hug hit me square in the solar plexus, all bones and warmth and need.

"I missed you," he mumbled against my shoulder. "When can I come back to your house?"

"Anytime," I said, brushing his hair from his forehead. "Are you feeling okay?"

"I have a fever," he said, sniffing. "They sent me home. I don't wanna go home. Can I go to your house instead of the closet? We can have tea and oranges."

Something cracked quietly inside me. "Sweetheart—"

"Sam!"

Marianne's voice cut through the air like the snap of a rubber band. She stood in the doorway, her eyes flicking between us. The warmth drained from Sam's face as fast as it had come.

"Mom, can I go to Aunt Tessa's?"

Marianne's mouth tightened. "Tessa isn't your aunt. She's not family."

Sam shrank back. The light in his eyes dimmed. He shuffled toward the desk again, small and silent.

"Marianne, I don't mind him visiting—"

"You're already dating his father. Isn't that enough?"

I blinked. "Sam, would you excuse your mother and me for a moment?"

Sam went back into the closet. Marianne and I went into her office.

"Hiro and I weren't really dating." At least not in this timeline. But we would be in a few months. Maybe even sooner now that I no longer needed Marianne for any paperwork. "Anyway, we called the fake dating off. I told my friends about the baby."

Her expression flickered—something like interest or maybe schadenfreude. "Did they accept it?"

I hesitated but saw no reason not to spit out the truth. "No."

Marianne made a small sound in her throat, half-laugh, half-sigh. It sounded smug. But what would she have to be smug about in my friendship situation?

"I'm not adopting the baby anymore," I said. "Lila's going to stay with me. We're going to raise the baby together."

The smug grin dropped, and Marianne narrowed her eyes at me. "That's not how this works. You can't just decide to change the plan. Lila is still a minor under state care. Any new arrangement will have to be reviewed, vetted, and approved. That means background checks, home visits, financial assessments—the whole process again."

Now it was my turn to deflate. I thought it would be a simple process without any documents necessary.

"Until Lila turns eighteen, she can't make legal decisions about custody or residence without CPS involvement. If she's living with you, that has to be documented."

Great. That meant I wouldn't be out from under Marianne's thumb anytime soon. I'd already seen her vindictive streak today when her son had hugged me and called me auntie. It was going to be a long few weeks until this new paperwork was done.

We gave Lila the news after she returned from the restroom. We sat side by side, a united front as Marianne droned on across from us like an inept general giving orders that we both doubted.

We were halfway across the parking lot when a familiar SUV pulled in. Hiro climbed out, sleeves rolled up, tie loose, a pencil still tucked behind his ear like an afterthought. The sight of him did something to my heartbeat—an involuntary yoga rhythm I hadn't meant to start.

"Professor Tanaka," Lila said with a grin, straightening a little.

"Lila," he greeted, warm as sunlight. "How are you holding up?"

She shrugged, shy but smiling. "Just have a baby dancing the chacha in my belly."

"That sounds about right."

Then he turned to me. The look that passed between us was quick, quiet, and entirely too much. I could see the same longing mirrored there. I was surprised the whole town couldn't see it, couldn't feel it. I wanted to step into him. I almost did.

"I'm here to pick up Sam," he said, his voice low, polite, familiar.

"Why don't you both stop by my place after? You know… if you'd like. I can have a pot of tea and oranges waiting for you on the back porch."

Hiro's mouth curved into a slow smile. "I think we'd like that."

CHAPTER TWENTY-EIGHT

The sun hung like a soft lantern over Stillwater, spilling pale light through the porch screens. Inside, Lila and Sam were asleep on the couch, their heads tipped toward opposite ends but their feet tangled in the middle. The tea on the table had gone cold, the orange slices picked clean to the rind. Hiro and I sat on the porch, the hum of the crickets filling the spaces where words might've gone.

"It's nice," he said quietly, eyes on the sleeping forms through the screen. "Seeing them like that."

I nodded. "Peaceful."

The kind of peace that used to fill my house after long days. Before everything changed. Before silence turned into something heavier.

I don't know why I started telling Hiro about Darnell. Maybe it was the tea or the easy steadiness of Hiro's presence. I told him about the way we'd met—me with my head in the clouds, Darnel with both feet planted firmly on the ground. How we'd built a life that felt steady and warm and enough. And how I'd thought love like that only came once.

"I didn't think I'd ever want to date again," I admitted. "It felt... disrespectful, somehow. Like moving forward meant leaving him behind."

Hiro leaned back, his hands resting on his knees. "When Marianne and I met, I thought—this is it. The person I'm going to grow old with. And then, somewhere along the way, it was like the girl I fell in love with just... evaporated. Same name, same face, but the spark was gone. That sounds cliché, but that's what it felt like. Like the light went out."

There was no bitterness in his voice, just quiet sadness. The kind that comes from trying too long to fix something that no longer fits.

I was surprised at how easy it was to talk about these people—our ghosts—to each other. There was no jealousy, no comparison. Just two souls quietly acknowledging that love had changed them in ways they hadn't expected.

When I stood to collect the empty cups, Hiro rose too. "Let me help."

Our fingers brushed—lightly, accidentally.

I looked up.

So did he.

The air between us thickened. Our breath mingled. Gravity pulled.

His hands were at my waist, firm and certain. Suddenly my back met the porch screen with a soft thrum that rattled through my ribs. The scent of tea and cedar wrapped around us, warm and familiar, anchoring me even as the ground seemed to tilt.

Then he kissed me.

The world didn't explode. It shifted—like a long-locked window finally letting in fresh air.

Hiro's mouth was warm against mine, a perfect blend of fire and restraint. There was a slow, deliberate pressure first, as though he was giving me space to pull away. When I didn't—when I leaned in —something in him gave way. His lips parted slightly, and heat curled through me.

His stubble grazed my skin, a rough whisper that made my breath stutter. Just for a dizzy heartbeat, I felt twenty again—barefoot on a summer night, heart reckless and unbroken, tasting possibility on someone else's lips.

But this wasn't Darnell.

That realization didn't hurt. Darnell had kissed me perfectly in his own steady, familiar way. This kiss—Hiro's kiss—was perfect too, but in an entirely different language.

Not better. Not worse. Just… his.

And God, I wanted to learn it. To lean in and deepen it, to see what the next breath, the next brush of lips, the next tilt of his head might unravel in me. It had been so long since I'd felt this kind of pull— gentle, curious, hungry.

Peace and excitement—two halves of the same inhale—passed between us like our bodies were sharing breath. When we finally broke apart, it was barely a separation at all. Hiro's forehead rested against mine, our noses brushing, our breaths shallow and mingling in the space of a sigh.

"I promised myself I'd wait," he said, voice rough.

"It doesn't matter," I whispered. "Marianne's already furious with me. We might as well give her something real to be mad about."

Hiro's lips twitched into the ghost of a smile. "That doesn't sound very Zen of you."

"I never said I was perfect."

"I would beg to differ." He brushed a thumb along my jaw. "What is it you want, Tessa?"

I said it before I could stop myself. "I want to be the one you come to when your shoulders get tired."

Hiro's grin was slow and devastating. "You've been checking out my shoulders?"

"Maybe." I slid my hands up his broad frame, feeling the strength beneath his shirt. "I had to see if the reputation was deserved."

He chuckled—a low, warm sound that melted into another kiss. This one was slower, deeper, full of everything we hadn't said yet. And then—

A knock at the door.

We froze, breath still tangled, hearts still racing. Hiro pulled back first, eyes wide, lips parted like he wanted to laugh and curse all at once.

The knock came again, firmer this time. Not the polite kind that belonged to neighbors or friends.

Inside, the living room light glowed soft and golden, spilling across the couch where Lila and Sam had been asleep. They were both up. Lila was moving Sam away from the door where two officers stood on my stoop.

"What's this about?" I demanded.

One of the officers stepped slightly forward, clearing his throat like he needed to soften what came next. When he lifted his gaze, recognition flickered between us.

Of course. Mark Vincent. He'd been a year behind me in school. Had carried a torch for Celia through all of sophomore year. Had asked me out once—very sweetly, very nervously—and I'd turned him down. He'd always been a little terrified of Lana. Most boys were. These days, he wielded that badge like it gave him authority he hadn't had as a teen. Now he stood on my porch in uniform, hat tucked under his arm, looking like he wished he were anywhere else.

"We have a report from this girls' parents. She's a minor, and she's been classified as a runaway. They've requested she be returned to their custody immediately."

Behind Mark, I saw them. Mr. and Mrs. Perez. Standing shoulder to shoulder like a wall of cold marble.

Mrs. Perez's lips were pressed into a thin, righteous line. Mr. Perez's arms were crossed, smug and sure.

"Lila Grace Perez, get your things right now."

I stepped in front of her. "She's safe here. I've been in contact with Child Protective Services. There's paperwork—"

"Paperwork doesn't change the law," Mr. Perez interrupted. "She's seventeen. She's our daughter."

Hiro appeared at my side then, quiet but steady, his presence grounding me. Sam clung to his leg, silent, eyes wide.

The other officer cleared his throat. "Ma'am, until the court determines otherwise, her parents retain full custody. I'm afraid she'll have to come with us."

I turned back to Lila. She looked impossibly small in that moment—hands trembling, eyes glistening, every inch of her shaking with fear.

"You can't make me go," she whispered, voice breaking. "Please, Tessa, don't let them—"

Mrs. Perez drew herself up, indignation sharp as glass. "We are her parents. We'll decide what's best for her and that child she's carrying."

That child.

Lila's hands flew protectively to her stomach. She started crying then—ragged, gasping sobs that tore through every ounce of composure I had left.

"Please," I said, my voice cracking. "At least let me call her caseworker. She's been placed here under supervision—"

Mark looked away.

But the officer shook his head. "That'll be handled through CPS in the morning. Right now, our orders are clear."

Lila's father stepped forward, his expression smug. "You see, young lady, this is what happens when you meddle in other people's families."

I wanted to scream. To grab Lila's hand and lock the door and tell them all to go to hell.

Instead, I did what I always did—I breathed. In. Out. In. It didn't help.

Lila turned to me, tears streaking her face. "They'll take the baby. I won't even get to hold her."

I reached for her, pulling her into my arms. "That will not happen. I will not let them keep either of you from me. I'll fight for you both. I promise."

She clung to me, sobbing, until the officer gently pried her away.

Hiro's jaw was clenched so tightly I saw the muscles ticking in his cheek. Sam hid his face against his father's side, trembling.

Mrs. Perez took Lila's arm, already talking over her sobs about repentance and forgiveness, about how everything would be "set right."

Lila didn't answer. She just looked back—eyes wide, wet, terrified—until the car door closed between us. The taillights glowed red as they pulled away, shrinking down the road until they disappeared.

CHAPTER TWENTY-NINE

The house was too quiet after they took her. The absence of sound hummed, heavy and wrong—like the air knew something sacred had been broken. Before I went quiet, I'd made every call I could think of. The police, who told me it was a family matter. Social Services, who said the file was being reviewed. Marianne, whose voicemail chirped a brisk "I'm out of the office until Monday."

Every door I knocked on closed with the same resounding echo: *There's nothing you can do.*

So I did what I always told my students not to do. I folded in on myself. I climbed into bed fully clothed with the scent of sandalwood still clinging to my sweater and let the ceiling blur. I'd spent my whole life helping people find peace. But in that moment, I couldn't find even a scrap of it for myself.

The room was dim, with the only light coming from the hallway. I heard soft footsteps. They hesitated before entering my bedroom, as though entering a sacred space.

The edge of the mattress dipped. A small hand brushed my back. I turned to find Sam there, solemn and earnest, a peeled orange in one hand and a mug of tea in the other. The tea was cloudy and pale, the kind of brew only a child could make—lukewarm and drowning in sugar.

"I made this for you. To make you feel better."

His small voice wavered at the edges, like he wasn't sure if he was allowed to comfort an adult.

I pushed myself upright, blinking fast to steady the blur in my vision. "Thank you, sweetheart."

Sam fidgeted, eyes darting down to the blanket covering my waist. "I'm sorry," he whispered. "I shouldn't have answered the door. It's my fault she's gone."

"Oh, Sam…" I set the mug aside and pulled him into my arms. He was all angles and sharp points. His small frame shook against me. "It's not your fault, honey. Not even a little bit."

He sniffled into my shoulder. "Her parents were mean. They yelled at her. I should've stopped them."

"Some parents…" My voice broke, and I had to breathe through it. "Some parents don't know how to love the way they should. But that's not something you can fix."

Sam pulled back just enough to look at me, his dark eyes too wise for his age. "My mom and dad fight sometimes. But Dad always finds a way to make it better." A small, brave certainty rang in his voice. "He'll make it better for you, too."

I wanted to believe him. Wanted to let that childlike faith patch the jagged place in my heart where Lila had been. Then I heard it—voices in the next room. Low, sharp, rising and falling like waves hitting rock.

Hiro's voice. And Marianne's.

The sound of it made Sam flinch. He turned toward the door, eyes wide.

I reached out, stilling him with a hand. "It's okay." Though it wasn't. "Stay here."

My pulse was already racing as I stood. Every breath was deeper and steadier than the last. I stepped out of my room and into whatever storm was waiting.

Their voices carried down the hallway before I

reached the end of it. Marianne's voice mainly. It was sharp, clipped, and too loud for a house that had been quiet only minutes before.

"You can't just insert yourself into every situation, Hiro. You're not her savior. You're barely keeping it together with your own kids."

"I'm not inserting myself," Hiro said, his voice low and steady, the same calm he used when speaking to Ellie after one of her storms. "I'm trying to help. That girl was safe here, and now she's not."

"Help?" Marianne snapped. "You mean Tessa was playing house, and you were just letting her? She's not fit to be a parent. She can't even decide what she wants. One minute she's adopting the baby, the next she's the girl's roommate. It's unstable."

Unfit. Indecisive. She said them like they were facts.

"Tessa will make an amazing mother," Hiro said. No hesitation. No defense. Just his belief in me.

Marianne's voice went lower now, dangerous. "You will not replace me with that woman as my children's mother."

Hiro didn't answer. That silence broke something in Marianne. I heard it in her next words. They were bitter and ugly.

"I don't want that woman anywhere near my children."

Hiro's tone stayed calm, but I could hear the steel underneath. "Then you'd better get used to being disappointed, because Tessa is going to be around them constantly. She's going to be in my life."

There was a pause—then the sound of a sharp intake of breath. "Don't you dare threaten me, Hiro. You think I won't sue for full custody?"

"Try it," he said simply.

I stepped forward before I even thought to.

That one sentence—quiet, certain, unflinching— seemed to shatter something in her. Marianne's voice broke when she spoke next, all pretense gone. "You'd really choose her over your own family?"

Hiro's sigh was quiet, pained. "I'm not choosing sides, Marianne. I'm choosing peace. And right now, you're making that impossible."

She turned then—and saw me. Her face went slack, pale. Then her mouth twisted into something cruel. "You think you can take care of someone else's child when you couldn't even have your own?"

Her words sliced through me like glass. She didn't yell them. She didn't need to. Marianne was excellent at finding the places that hurt the most.

She brushed past me and out the door, slamming

it behind her. The sound echoed down the hallway long after she was gone.

I stayed frozen for a moment, still reeling, until I heard Hiro exhale. When I looked at him, he looked... hollow. His shoulders slumped, eyes shadowed with exhaustion and something deeper—shame, maybe, or just heartbreak stretched too thin.

"I'm sorry," he said quietly. "For her. For all of this."

I shook my head. "You don't have to apologize for someone else's cruelty."

Still, he looked like a man carrying too much. I crossed the room before I could talk myself out of it and wrapped my arms around him.

Hiro went rigid at first—like no one had touched him in years. Then, slowly, he softened, his breath leaving in a shaky sigh against my hair.

I didn't say anything. Just held him, breathing him in. When he finally spoke, his voice was rough. "I'll make this right. With Marianne. With Lila. We'll get her back."

CHAPTER THIRTY

I didn't sleep alone that night.

Hiro was a steady warmth against my back, his breath slow and even, his arm slung around my waist like an anchor. He didn't try anything. Just kissed my temple once, soft and reverent, before settling behind me. I told myself to stay awake, to memorize the weight of him, the feel of safety I hadn't realized I'd been starving for. But the exhaustion pulled me under.

When I woke, sunlight was pooling through the curtains in my bedroom. The air smelled like jasmine and citrus. He'd made me my favorite tea. Had I told him that? Or had he just known? I rolled over to ask him, but the other side of the bed was empty.

He was gone.

Instead, Lana stood at the dresser in her fiercest navy business suit, heels off, hair pulled back like a woman preparing for battle. She was stirring a honey stick into a steaming mug of what had to be jasmine tea.

"Get up, sleepyhead," she said, setting the cup on my nightstand. "We've got motions to file."

I blinked, still half-dreaming. "Lana? What—where's Hiro?"

"He had a class to teach. He didn't want to leave, but I convinced him the cavalry had arrived. You'd think that man didn't know what a village was."

I took the mug my bestie made for me. My lips immediately went to the rim, and I took a sip. It was perfect.

"Your boy toy filled us in," Lana said matter-of-factly, as if late-night crisis calls were just another Tuesday. "He told us what happened with Lila and her parents, said you needed to rest. So we took over."

"We?"

Celia breezed in a second later, balancing a tray with croissants, jams, and an entire pot of tea. Her hair tamed into a sleek ponytail. It was another sign that my friends were officially in damage-control mode.

I sat up slowly, still foggy, still not sure I deserved their efficiency, their care.

Celia set the tray in front of me, perched on the edge of the bed, and gave me that look—equal parts stern and maternal. "You look like hell, honey. Eat something before you try to fix the world."

The perfectly balanced yin and yang circle inside of me cracked then. All the composure I'd been holding on to like a lifeline dissolved under the warmth of their presence. There were no lectures. No *why didn't you tell us?* No *what were you thinking?* Just two women who had shown up, as they always did, when I needed them most. I hadn't had many crises in my life, but when they came, Lana and Celia were never far behind.

The tears came before I could stop them. I pressed a hand to my mouth, embarrassed, but Celia just passed me a napkin and said, "There she goes. About time."

Lana sat beside me, tucking her legs under herself. "We've already drafted the paperwork. I can file a petition against Lila's parents for neglect. It's going to take some time, but we'll get it done."

Her gaze caught mine—fierce, unwavering. "We're going to get your family back, Tess."

The words hit deep. *Your family.* I hadn't even let myself think that far ahead. But hearing it—hearing the person on this planet who knew me best say it—made something bloom in my chest. A fragile, trembling hope.

I nodded, unable to speak past the lump in my throat. I reached for their hands, one on each side, and just breathed. For the first time since that knock at the door, I let myself sink into the knowledge that I wouldn't have to face this alone.

But it wasn't that simple.

Emotional neglect is hard to prove. That's what Lana said as she paced my kitchen, her heels clicking like a metronome of frustration. I'd never seen her so undone by a case—not even during her divorce. She'd drafted motions, pulled statutes, even called in favors from old contacts at the courthouse. None of it changed the simple, cruel truth: Lila's parents still had every legal right to her.

They could withhold her phone. They could dictate where she lived, who she saw, and what doctor she went to. They could decide if she kept her baby. Or not.

The thought made my stomach twist.

I'd seen those parents—tight smiles and venom beneath the surface, righteousness sharp enough to cut. They didn't love Lila. They wanted to control her. And somehow, the law still sided with them.

Lana had said it over breakfast this morning: "The system's built to keep families together, not tear them apart."

I wanted to scream. Instead, I smiled and said I understood. I always understand.

Now sitting alone in the yoga studio, I stared at the candle flickering on the altar and tried to breathe through the ache. Every exhale carried a wish I didn't believe in anymore. *Bring her back. Keep her safe. Let her know she's loved.*

Lana was doing everything she could—filing for neglect, pushing for emergency review, building a case that Lila's parents were unfit. But the state wanted proof, not feelings. They wanted evidence of danger. Not bruised hearts or clipped wings.

Meanwhile, Marianne was making everything worse. She'd been reassigned to another department after Hiro complained about a conflict of interest. But she still had friends in CPS. Friends who "lost" paperwork. Who "misplaced" files. Who whispered that I wasn't stable, that I'd changed my story too many times.

One week I wanted to adopt the baby. The next, I wanted to take in Lila. Now I wanted both. And apparently that made me unfit. The irony would've been funny if it didn't make me want to break something.

I pressed my palms together in my lap, trying to center. "Root to rise," I whispered to myself. "Ground, then grow." But my grounding felt shaky these days. Every phone call from Lana was another obstacle:

"They're lawyering up."

"They're saying you influenced her decision to keep the baby."

"They're claiming you encouraged her to run away."

Each accusation chipped away at something I hadn't realized was fragile—my faith in people, in fairness, in the idea that good intentions mattered.

Hiro tried to keep me steady. He showed up every evening in person or on the phone after the kids were asleep. He didn't tell me to calm down or be patient. He just let me talk. Sometimes he'd read legal paperwork over my shoulder, brow furrowed in concentration. Other times, he'd make me tea and hold my hand, his thumb tracing circles on my skin like a wordless mantra.

But even his calm couldn't soothe the growing dread. Because while we were filing motions and waiting for judges, Lila was somewhere else. Somewhere she didn't want to be. Somewhere she was alone.

The nights were the worst. I'd wake up to silence —no soft footsteps, no kettle hissing, no sound of her humming absentmindedly as she did her homework. Just the echo of a house that had been full and now wasn't.

"We're working the system," Lana would remind me. But it didn't feel like progress. It felt like drowning in molasses. And still, I couldn't stop trying.

I left messages with Social Services every morning. I sent gentle texts to Lila's number, even though I knew her parents had taken her phone. I kept her room clean, her favorite mug on the counter, a folded blanket waiting on the couch—like she'd just stepped out for a walk and would be back any minute.

Some nights, I caught myself praying. Not to anyone in particular. Just to something bigger, someone that might listen.

Please. Don't let her think I gave up.

Because I hadn't. I wouldn't. Not when the world had already taught the girl that she was disposable.

Lana said it could take weeks, maybe months, to get a hearing.

Celia said to be patient.

Hiro said to trust the process.

But I'd built a life out of teaching people to let go —and now I was realizing that love means the opposite.

Sometimes, you have to hold on.

Even when it hurts.

Even when it's impossible.

Even when the law tells you not to.

CHAPTER THIRTY-ONE

I was halfway through sorting receipts for the studio—an exercise in patience disguised as bookkeeping—when my phone buzzed across the counter.

Hiro Tanaka.

It had been two weeks since Lila was taken. Two weeks since the first time Hiro kissed me on my back porch, soft and sure and devastating in its gentleness.

Two weeks since everything in my life had split cleanly into Before and After.

In those fourteen days, Hiro and I had spoken every single one of them. Sometimes for five minutes between his classes, sometimes for twenty on my lunch break, sometimes late at night when the house was too quiet and the ache of missing people kept me awake.

We didn't see each other nearly as much as either of us wanted. It was some big certifications test for his students. Every time I called, I heard the scratch of his pencil, the weariness in his voice, the way he apologized for being distracted even though he gave me his full attention for the brief moments we stole.

I was buried in paperwork and consults and the slow, maddening grind of trying to bring a girl home who never should've been taken in the first place. But when we did see each other...

It was like stepping into a bubble, sealed off from everything loud and ugly and unfair about the world. Sometimes we talked—about his students, about my classes, about Sam's newfound love of sea otters. Sometimes we didn't talk at all. Sometimes we just sat together, shoulder to shoulder, breathing the same air.

Sometimes we kissed—slow, lingering, unhurried kisses that made time lose its edges. He never rushed. He never pushed for more. With Hiro, nothing felt urgent. Nothing felt stolen. He made time expand around us in a way I'd forgotten was possible—like life paused, the lake stilled, and all the questions and fears that clawed at my ribs went quiet.

In those moments, everything was right. Lila was safe in her room. His kids were laughing out on the porch. And we were together, in whatever fragile, precious way together meant right now.

That feeling kept me afloat.

Which is probably why my heart did its ridiculous hummingbird flutter when my phone buzzed across the counter. Just seeing his name loosened the tension in my neck.

"Hey." His voice was low and warm, that familiar blend of steadiness and fatigue. "I'm going to be late tonight. One of my students asked for an extra meeting. She's struggling, and…" He trailed off, the way he did when his sense of duty pulled him in two directions at once. "Then I have to swing by the sitter to get the kids."

"I can get them," I said quickly. "If that helps. I'll take them to your house and keep them company until you're home."

Hiro hesitated. "Tessa, you don't have to—"

"I know. I want to."

A small sigh came through the line—part relief,

part surrender. "All right. Thank you. How about I get the sitter to drop them off to my house to save you a trip? She doesn't live far. I'll leave my spare key at the college front desk."

"Perfect," I said.

I tidied the last of my paperwork into a neat, futile stack and headed out. The campus was quiet this time of day, the buildings glowing in that honeyed, late-afternoon light that made even brick look soft. I walked into the administration office, introduced myself to the receptionist, and asked for Hiro's key. She handed it to me and went back to her computer.

When I walked out of the office, Hiro was leaning against a bulletin board in the hallway.

Before I could say a word, he reached for me—one hand at the back of my neck, the other at my waist—and kissed me. It wasn't rushed or hesitant. It was warm and sure, the kind of kiss that dissolved the day in an instant.

He pulled back, smiling, eyes bright behind his glasses. "I couldn't resist," he said quietly. "I just needed to see you. Hold you for a second."

I grinned up at him, heart tripping over itself. My gaze lingered, greedy, tracing over the details I'd come to crave. The pencil tucked behind his ear—always there, like part of his anatomy—sat angled and snug, ready for whatever note he needed to capture next. It made him look scholarly and devastatingly capable all at once.

Gray threaded through the hair at his temples. Those little flashes of silver made me want to smooth my fingers through them, to press my palm there as if I could absorb some piece of his quiet strength.

The lines at the corners of his eyes—deep, worried creases that had been carved by years of responsibility and too many nights spent soothing other people's storms—gathered when he smiled. Those lines made me ache. Made me want to soften them with my thumb. Made me want to take on some of the weight that caused them.

Hiro smiled down at me, like he knew exactly what I was thinking. He lifted his hand, cradling my face. His thumb smoothed the lines at the corner of my left eye, and I melted into him.

Kissing him wasn't going to be enough much longer. Not when my body leaned toward his without permission. Not when every part of me hummed with the quiet, undeniable truth: I didn't just want him beside me on porches.

I wanted him in my bed.

In my life.

In whatever future waited on the other side of all this chaos.

"How are you holding up?" he asked.

"Lana thinks she's found something. But it could destroy Lila's parents. I'm not sure if I want to go that far."

He nodded, thoughtful. He didn't push, didn't tell me what I should do. He just listened, the way he always did. That quiet patience of his unraveled me more than any touch could. And that's when I knew it.

I loved him.

I hadn't told him yet. I hadn't even slept with him yet, which Lana found absolutely tragic. But I was certain of it. I loved this man who met me where I was and never asked me to rush.

Hiro glanced at the clock and sighed. "I need to get back for my meeting. But we'll talk tonight, okay?"

"Okay."

He leaned in for another kiss. It was just a quick brush of his lips over mine, but it left me breathless, anyway. Then he was gone, walking down the hall with that easy stride, leaving the air around me humming.

THE DRIVE to his house felt strangely intimate. I'd been there before but never alone. The late sun caught in the windows, lighting up fingerprints and smudges and the kind of lived-in clutter that said children live here. A basket of mismatched socks by the stairs. Crayon drawings taped crookedly to the wall. An open book on the coffee table with a crayon tucked inside like a secret.

The doorbell rang, and the babysitter stood on the porch with a tired smile. Sam's face lit up the second he saw me. He ran straight into my arms, all warmth and motion and that little-boy smell of grass and soap.

"Miss Tessa!" he said, muffled against my shoulder.

"Hey, sweetheart."

Behind him, Ellie was in full meltdown—tiny fists balled, face red, voice pitched to a shriek.

The babysitter sighed. "She didn't want to put her shoes on. Then she didn't want me to help. You know how it is."

I nodded. I did.

The sitter's gaze flicked down my body—barefoot, yoga pants, messy bun—and I could practically hear the story she'd tell the rest of the town. They'd gotten wind of the entire sordid story of my relationship and my desire to alter my family status. I smiled anyway, thanked her, and shut the door behind her.

Inside, the house felt smaller with all that emotion contained in it. Ellie's screams echoed off the walls, and Sam flinched like each one landed on him.

"It's okay," I said to him, then turned to his sister. "Ellie, honey, what are you trying to do?"

"I can do it myself!" Ellie cried, small fingers knotted in the stubborn loops of her shoelaces. She sat on the bench inside the foyer, face flushed, breath hiccupping in indignation. The laces were a tangled mess—two limp worms she kept yanking in every direction but the right one.

Sam hovered at her shoulder like a shadow ready to leap into action. His hands twitched at his sides, his whole body pulled taut with the urge to fix, to help, to shield.

I brushed my fingers lightly across his arm. "Let her try."

He looked up at me—wide, uncertain eyes that

carried far too much responsibility for someone his age. I held his gaze until the tension in his shoulders eased, just a hair.

"You don't have to solve everything, sweetheart. Let her figure this one out."

Sam swallowed, then nodded, stepping back a pace. I could almost see the gears turning inside him —habit arguing with hope.

Behind us, Ellie grunted and tugged, her frustration growing louder with every failed attempt. "It's not WORKING!" she wailed.

"I'm sure you'll figure out it, sweetie," I said calmly, shifting my attention to Sam. "So Sam. What should we do while we wait for your father to get home?"

He blinked, thrown off balance by the redirect. "Um… can we make tea? Dad got some flower tea like you have."

Hiro had bought jasmine tea? Why did that not shock me. The man was forever thinking about others. I loved that I was one of his others.

While we talked, Ellie kept wrestling her shoelaces, her breaths turning sharp and uneven. But without Sam swooping in, something shifted. Her tantrum softened into focus—small brow knitting, little fingers fumbling with intention instead of panic.

Finally, she let out a hiccupping sob. "I need help."

I reached in gently. "Okay. I can—"

"No!" she cried, jerking back. "Sam. I want Sam's help."

Sam stepped forward. But he didn't tie his sister's shoelaces for her. He crouched down and untied his own laces. "First make an X. No, like this… yeah. Then, pull one side under. No, you do it. I'm just telling you."

Ellie sniffled her way through the motions, trying, failing, trying again. At one point she started to cry again, little face reddening. Sam's hands twitched like he wanted to take over—but he didn't.

"You've got it, Ellie. Just twist it… yeah, like that."

And finally—miraculously—she looped, pulled, tightened.

"I DID IT!" Ellie shouted, triumphant, lifting her foot high like a trophy.

Sam beamed—pure pride, pure relief. I wished Hiro was here to see it. This—this right here—was what Hiro was building in them. What I wanted to help build, too. Small moments of letting them grow by letting them do it themselves.

My entire body straightened at that thought. It was like a gong went off in my head and reverberated down to my toes. Watching Sam help his sister tie her shoes herself had shown me the solution to all my problems.

Once I made the kids snacks, I pulled out my cell phone and dialed.

"Hey, babe," said Lana's voice.

"What if Lila was emancipated?"

CHAPTER THIRTY-TWO

I sat near the back of the courthouse, hands clasped in my lap, trying to breathe evenly. Lana stood at the front, calm and razor-sharp in her navy suit, the picture of poise and purpose. I'd seen her argue cases before, but never one that mattered this much.

Hiro sat beside me, our knees touching on the hard wooden bench. At some point—maybe during the judge's instructions, maybe during the testimony from the first witness—his hand had found mine. His thumb rested against the inside of my wrist, a steady, grounding rhythm.

We weren't doing anything inappropriate, but the way the courtroom staff kept glancing at us, we might as well have been making out on the judge's bench.

The bailiff, Keith "Don't Call Me Kenny" Walters, kept cutting looks our way. I'd gone to school with his sister. She'd been the kind of girl who baked cookies for people she wanted to impress. Kenny… had always been the opposite. He didn't care what anyone thought, and he loved to tell everyone's business.

The clerk, Mrs. Porter—no relation to Bo but a longtime friend of my mother's—was even worse. Thin lips pressed tight, eyes darting over the edge of her bifocals like binoculars. My mother and she had been on the outs for years, ever since some argument over a church committee election. From the look she exchanged with Kenny, I knew one thing for certain: News of me and Hiro would be all over town—and grossly exaggerated—in about five minutes. Never mind the no-cell-phones in court edict. Gossip moved faster than LTE in Stillwater Springs.

I squeezed Hiro's hand a little tighter, both for courage and to remind myself that none of this—the stares, the whispers preparing to be born—was what mattered.

Lila sat at the petitioner's table, shoulders drawn tight, her belly pressing against the edge. She looked small and impossibly young, the way all seventeen-year-olds look when they're pretending not to be afraid. Across from her, her parents sat side by side with pressed suits and polite smiles.

Every so often, Lila glanced my way. I met her gaze and held it. *You're safe,* I willed the look to say. *We're here. You're not alone.*

Lana had the stage. "Mr. and Mrs. Perez, the court understands your daughter left home a month ago. Is that correct?"

Her father leaned forward, his tone syrupy and controlled. "She wasn't kicked out, Your Honor. She left of her own accord. We simply wanted her to follow house rules."

Beside him, Lila's mother nodded tightly. "We've been worried sick since she ran away."

The lies slid from their tongues like oil. My stomach twisted. Lila's knuckles whitened on the edge of the table.

Lana stepped forward, her voice measured. "Am I to understand that your house rules included denying your daughter medical care, restricting her access to school, and refusing to allow her to contact Social Services after discovering her pregnancy?"

Her mother's lips thinned. "We were protecting her."

"From what?" Lana pressed.

"From herself."

The judge's brow furrowed.

I caught movement at the side of the room—Marianne, sitting stiff-backed near the witness bench. Her hair was perfect, her expression carved from stone. She avoided my gaze until she didn't. When her eyes finally met mine, I saw it—the flicker of guilt, the recognition. She knew. She could end this. The question was would she?

Marianne was called upon next. "Ms. Tanaka, as a representative of Child Protective Services, you've had contact with the minor. Would you share your professional assessment of the petitioner's home environment prior to this filing?"

Marianne hesitated, fingers tightening around her notes. "I conducted a home visit when Ms. Perez was residing with her parents. There were... concerns. Emotional volatility. Limited parental support. It's my understanding Ms. Perez was subsequently asked to leave the home."

The judge raised an eyebrow. "Asked to leave, or told to?"

Marianne exhaled through her nose, each word sounding torn from her throat. "Told to."

Lila's father muttered something under his breath.

The judge leaned forward. "And where did Ms. Perez go after that?"

"She stayed temporarily with Ms. Tessa Bloom," Marianne said, glancing at me like the name tasted bitter. "Ms. Bloom operates a yoga and wellness studio in Stillwater Springs. She has a stable home, no criminal record, and adequate financial resources."

The judge nodded. "Do you consider Ms. Bloom's home to be a safe environment for both the petitioner and her child?"

Marianne's jaw worked. "Yes," she said finally. "It's stable."

Lana turned back toward Lila. "Your Honor, Ms. Perez has demonstrated maturity and independence. She's attending community college, maintaining employment at Ms. Bloom's studio, and preparing for motherhood. We ask the court to recognize her right to self-determination."

The judge shifted her gaze to Lila. "Miss Perez, I've heard from your attorney, your parents, and Child Protective Services. Now I want to hear from you. Why do you believe emancipation is in your best interest?"

Lila took a shaky breath. Her voice trembled at first but grew steadier with each word. "Because I don't see eye to eye with my parents. They think love means control, and I can't live like that. I don't want to raise my baby in fear. I want to raise her with people who love us both."

Her eyes found mine again. "I want to live with Tessa. She helps me feel like I can be the kind of woman—and the kind of mother—I want to be."

My heart caught in my throat. The judge's pen stilled mid-note.

After a long, quiet moment, the judge set the papers down. "The court finds sufficient evidence that Ms. Perez is capable of managing her own affairs and that emancipation is in her best interest. The petition is granted."

Lila gasped softly, her hand flying to her mouth. Lana exhaled for the first time in what felt like hours. I pressed my palms together and closed my eyes, letting the relief wash through me.

When I opened them again, Lila was standing before me. I enveloped her in a hug that I was determined never to let her out of. I felt a kick from the bump on her belly as though the baby was on board with that notion. Hiro was at my back, grinning down at us. Lana was standing in front of me, ready to ride or die like always. I looked up and caught a ray of sunshine spreading a faint rainbow on the window and knew that my husband was giving me his blessing.

CHAPTER THIRTY-THREE

The sunlight peeked through the resort's gauzy curtains in soft, golden stripes, warm against the sheets tangled around my legs. I stretched—slowly, luxuriously—and the linens slipped over my bare skin like a whispered secret. Muscles I hadn't used in years hummed their quiet protests, the delicious kind you carry home from a good yoga session or… well. What Hiro and I had been doing since we checked in last night.

It was astonishing how two nights away could feel like an entire season of rest.

Celia had called it a babymoon, though technically I wasn't the baby mama about to give birth, and Hiro wasn't the father—not biologically, anyway.

Lana had just smiled her knowing smile and shoved a family-sized (pun had to be intended) pack of condoms into my hands with the force of a woman who had raised three kids, survived heartbreak, and knew a thing or two about people who desperately needed to get out of their own lives for a minute.

So we went.

Somehow, stepping into the quiet mountain resort felt like exhaling for the first time in months.

It didn't matter that we were only an hour from Stillwater—far enough to shed the weight of hearings and paperwork, close enough that Hiro could still check the parenting app he shared with Marianne. She had been, let's call it civil these past few weeks. Not only did she have an extra babysitter for the nights she wanted to, let's call it work late, but I had even more babysitters available so that Hiro and I never had to call her for an emergency sit. Though we called our babysitters our community and not the hired help. If Marianne would remove a few of the chips off her shoulder, we'd have gladly welcomed her in.

Well, Celia would. Maybe Lila. But Lana could hold a grudge.

I smiled into the pillow, letting the quiet of the

room settle into my chest. It reminded me of the first deep breath after meditation—the one that feels like it reaches all the way to the bones.

I wasn't alone. I could feel him behind me, the warmth of his body tucked along the curve of mine, an arm draped heavily over my waist. Hiro slept quietly, like a man who had wrestled his thoughts long into the night and finally surrendered.

His breath stirred the back of my neck, and I shivered under it. Not from cold. From recognition. I'd forgotten how it felt to wake up beside someone.

I stretched, slow and indulgent, and the movement roused him. I felt his fingers flex against my stomach, then trail lightly along my hip, tracing me as if he needed a reminder that I was real.

"Tessa," he murmured, voice rough with sleep.

The sound of my own name—spoken like that—sent heat unspooling through me. I rolled toward him. His hair was mussed, his glasses abandoned somewhere on the nightstand, his eyes warm with a softness I still didn't know how to hold without trembling.

"Morning," I whispered.

He studied me for a long, quiet moment. Not in the way men do when they're taking inventory but

the way someone looks when they want to memorize a feeling.

"When I wake, I've forgotten how beautiful you
are."

This man. How could any woman let a man like
this go? Didn't matter. Losers weepers, because I had
found him, and I was determined to never lose him.
Hell, I hadn't even let either of us leave the room
since we got here. It was a rare time I had him all to
myself, and I was not going to take these precious
hours lightly.

Sleep. Touch. Laughter. Food delivered to the
door and left untouched far too long. More sleep.
More touch.

It felt like we'd stolen time. Like we'd slipped into
a pocket of the universe where nothing existed but
breath and skin and the quiet, reverent way Hiro
said my name.

"Are you sore?"

A smile tugged at my lips. "Deliciously."

The sound he made at that—half groan, half
laughter—went straight through me. He shifted
closer, tracing a fingertip along the slope of my hip,
the touch feather-light but full of promise.

"Well," he murmured, "in cases like this… it might
be best to reboot the system."

I raised an eyebrow. "Reboot?"

"There must be an off switch somewhere," he said, amusement threading through his voice even as his fingertips followed a path down my waist, leaving tiny sparks along my skin. "Let me see if I can find it."

"Hiro—"

But he was already sliding under the covers, his warmth moving lower, his breath brushing places that made my stomach clench and my thoughts scatter.

A shiver chased up my spine. Somewhere beneath the sheets, I felt his smile.

"Ah," he said softly. "Found it."

My breath caught. The world tilted. Sensation bloomed in hot, slow waves that made my toes curl against the mattress.

Hiro pressed the button with his tongue. He encircled it with his lips. He tugged at it with his entire mouth. I rebooted all right. My heels dug into the mattress as my back arched off the bed.

"I'm pretty sure that's the get-off button," I managed, my voice already fraying at the edges.

His laugh vibrated through me, wicked and tender at once. "My mistake," he murmured. "Better press it again, then."

And when he did, the whole room dissolved into light.

For a long moment after, the world didn't come back. Not the bed beneath us, or the soft rush of mountain wind against the windows, or even the faint distant sound of water moving through the lodge's stone fountain.

Just him inside of me. Just me wrapped around him. Our breaths, tangled and uneven, floating in the quiet shimmer of what we'd just shared.

Hiro was still moving inside me in slow, instinctive aftershocks, his forehead pressed to mine, eyes somehow both fierce and undone. I cupped his jaw, feeling the stubble scrape gently against my palm. His eyes stayed locked on mine—unflinching, unguarded, reverent in a way that let me know I was loved.

And then he let go. A soft, breaking sigh against my mouth as he buried his face in my neck, as if he could hide the way he trembled. I held him close, my legs curling around him, my arms lifting to cradle the back of his head.

When my own release hit again, it was not fire or lightning. It was warmth. A profound softening. A quiet knowing. Like I was exhaling for the first time after holding my breath for years.

When it passed, we collapsed into each other, limbs tangled, hearts still racing.

He whispered my name like a prayer. I said his like a promise.

I didn't know how long we clung together. Minutes, maybe. A suspended lifetime. The room remained hushed around us, like even the walls understood that something sacred had just shifted.

There was so much love in my chest it almost frightened me. I'd felt this with Darnell. It was the same but different. I knew how lucky I was to have found not one but two soul mates in this lifetime.

There was room in me for more. So much more. For Lila, bravely rebuilding her whole future. For the baby she carried. For Sam's gentle heart and Ellie's lightning spirit. Even if life allowed it someday for Marianne… if she ever set her bitterness down.

Right now, all that space belonged to one person.

"Hiro," I whispered.

He lifted his head, eyes still heavy with emotion. He looked almost dazed. "You okay?"

I nodded, brushing my thumb along the line of gray at his temple. "I'm perfect."

"Good. Because I—" His voice cracked slightly,

and he closed his eyes for a beat. "I didn't think I'd ever… feel this again. With anyone."

"Me neither." I kissed his temple, then his cheek, then the soft place beneath his ear. "Roll over."

He blinked, confused. "What?"

"I want to be the big spoon."

His laugh was low and disbelieving, the sound vibrating through both of us. "Okay," he said, voice rough and tender at the same time. "Okay."

He shifted onto his side, back to my front. I scooted closer, fitting my body to his long frame. My arm draped over his waist, my knees tucked behind his. I pressed my face between his shoulder blades, inhaling the warm, steady scent of him— clean skin, cedar, a hint of the tea we'd spilled on the sheets.

I felt him relax. Not halfway. Entirely. Like a man exhaling a burden he'd carried too long.

His hand found mine where it rested over his heart. He threaded our fingers together and squeezed—once, strong and sure.

Our breaths synced naturally, falling into the same slow cadence. In. Out. In. Out.

We didn't sleep. We didn't talk. We simply lay there, wrapped around each other, existing in the first perfect peace either of us had felt in years.

Something small and bruised and long-protected opened.

I thought of Darnell.

His steady warmth, his soft laugh, the way he'd held my hand through both sickness and fear. Loving him had shaped me. Grief had been my shadow, my companion, my ballast. I'd survived by learning stillness, by teaching peace, by convincing myself I was whole even when half of me was missing.

But here, with Hiro's heartbeat steady under my palm, I realized the strangest, most beautiful truth: I wasn't moving on from Darnell. I was carrying him forward—into a life he would've wanted for me.

A life where I wasn't alone.

A life where healing didn't mean forgetting… it meant opening again.

Hiro shifted slightly, adjusting our joined hands. He didn't say anything, but I felt every unspoken thing in the way he breathed—like a man who had spent years bracing for impact, and finally, finally found a place to land.

I thought of Marianne, of their fractured past, of the heavy way he carried responsibility and kindness like twin weights across his shoulders. Of the nights he'd stayed awake worrying about his children. Of the quiet way he always put himself last. Of all the hurt he had swallowed because he believed it was easier than hurting someone else.

But this moment—this soft, quiet, sacred moment—I could feel him setting those burdens down too.

Here.

With me.

Not because I healed him and not because he healed me. But because we had walked through our separate storms… and somehow ended up at the same patch of sunlight.

I pressed myself closer, fitting my body to his. Our breaths aligned. Our hearts steadied. Outside, the world kept turning—messy, unpredictable, beautiful.

In here, in the cocoon of our tangled limbs and shared warmth, I understood the truth of it:

We weren't just healing.

We were healed.

Together.

Get ready for the next story in the
Stillwater Springs collection!

Next up? A divorced mom enters the dregs of the
dating pool, and when she starts to drown she
begins to wonder
if the ex-husband who's always close by when she
needs him might be the one who got away.

Find out in *Still Mine,*
Book Four in the Still Water Springs
later life romances!

ABOUT THE AUTHOR

Jem Johnson writes small-town, big-heart romances about women over forty rediscovering desire, purpose, and the power of second chances. A firm believer that it's never too late to fall in love—or finally choose yourself—Jem crafts emotionally rich stories filled with family ties, lifelong friendships, and slow-burn chemistry that simmers through every season of life. When she's not writing, you'll find her people-watching in a coffee shop, filling her planner with too many stickers, or plotting her next fictional Jubilee. *Stillwater Springs* is her love letter to women who've done the work... and are ready to feel alive again.

Visit my web store for steals, deals, and access to my books before they're on retailers! https://jemjohnsonbooks.com/

ALSO BY JEM JOHNSON

STILLWATER SPRINGS
Still the One
Still Got It
Still Healing
Still Mine
Still Yours
Still Home